I0451225

# BREWED WITH LOVE

KIMBERLY ROSE JOHNSON

Brewed with Love
Published by Sweet Rose Press
U.S.A.
Copyright © 2017 Kimberly R. Johnson

Cover design: Jackie Castle, www.CastleCreations.com

All rights reserved. Except for use in any review, the reproduction or utilization of this work in whole or in part in any form by any electronic, mechanical or other means, now known or hereinafter invented, including xerography, photocopying and recording, or in any information storage or retrieval system, is forbidden without the written permission from the author.

This is a work of fiction. Names, characters, places and incidents are either the product of the author's imagination or are used fictitiously, and any resemblance to actual persons, living or dead, business establishments, events or locales is entirely coincidental.

# Acknowledgements

This story was originally published in *Love in Mistletoe Springs*. I had such a good time writing this novella. It was quite an experience putting together a continuing story with each story standing alone. What follows is my slightly tweaked contribution to that collection. I hope you enjoy *Brewed with Love*.

# 1

This place was his final hope. If the new owner of Main Street Java didn't say yes, he was out of options. "Excuse me." Bryan Grant nudged past a group of women crowding the entryway to the coffee shop and stepped inside. He breathed in deeply the rich smell of brewed coffee as he removed his sunglasses and surveyed the room. The place had been modernized with new tables and chairs and a fresh coat of deep orange paint on one wall. He'd liked the shop just the way it had always been but appreciated the improvements. The rustic brick wall to the left was the perfect backdrop for a stage, but from what he'd heard it would take some talking to convince the girl he'd once had a crush on of that.

Annika Cooke didn't allow live bands in her shop, and according to his buddy she didn't care for musicians in general. He hoped to win her over once she heard his story.

"Stacy, will you take a few minutes and bus the tables?" The longhaired brunette, whose beautiful blue eyes he remembered so clearly from her summer visits, spoke softly to Stacy James, a longtime resident of Mistletoe Springs.

Stacy grabbed a rag and a tub to clear white coffee cups and plates from a table. It looked like he'd chosen a good time to stop in since there was no line and only one table was occupied. Main Street Java re-opened this past week after the death of the old owner had forced it to close. Bryan sauntered to the counter and flashed his best smile at Annika. "Hi there."

She offered a polite grin. "What can I get for you?"

"A large coffee and a few minutes of your time?" This might be harder than he thought, since she clearly had no memory of him.

Her gaze shot to his. "Does that line work with all the ladies?" She poured his coffee into a tall paper cup and clicked the lid in place.

His face heated. "Ah, no. I'm not trying to hit on you." He handed her the exact change. Sure, Annika had been a summer crush between his freshman and sophomore years of high school, but he'd sworn off women after Mandy rejected his proposal. He wasn't going there again.

"Oh." She pressed her lips together.

"Do you have a few minutes to talk?"

A wary look filled her eyes. "About what?"

"I'm looking for a place where my band can practice."

She shook her head, and soft waves caressed her

cheeks. "Sorry."

"Please, hear me out." He was desperate, and this coffee house was the only location in town with a decent facility that he hadn't already asked. "We used to practice in my buddy's garage, but his wife kicked us out."

"And you think that information will sell me on the idea of you practicing here?" She crossed her arms giving him a look that said he'd lost the battle before it had even begun.

He took a deep breath and let it out slowly. "Okay, point taken, but I forgot to mention they have a newborn."

"Ah. Now I see. But I don't understand why you want to practice here." Her brows scrunched. "Surely there are other places in town better suited to your needs."

He held up his cup. "Do you mind if we sit?"

She looked around the space then back at him. "I guess, but just for a few minutes. We're about to close, and I have cleaning to do."

"I'll make it fast. Promise." He set the cup on the nearest table for two, pulled out a chair for her, then eased onto the hard wooden seat. She sat, back ramrod straight, hands laced on the tabletop across from him. As a teen she'd been reserved, and it was one of the qualities that drew her to him, but now it just made him nervous.

"Okay, here's the deal. I don't have a garage, and the other guys can't practice at their places because they live in apartments."

"What about renting the community center?"

He rubbed his fingers together. "Too expensive."

"A school?"

"Same."

"Another business here in town?"

"Nope. I tried. The old owner of Main Street Java used to have an amateur night on Fridays. It was called Open Mic Night." He pointed to the brick wall. "She pushed the tables away from the brick wall and set up a stage. It was a very popular event."

"Yeah, well, my aunt was a sucker for entertainers." Her face softened for a moment then went serious. "Although I appreciate your situation, I'm not my aunt. I don't even know you or anything about you. You could be a mass murderer for all I know."

He chuckled in spite of the gravity of her words. "You're wrong. You do know me, but Stacy can vouch for me." He turned toward the blonde and raised his voice slightly. "Stacy, will you tell your boss that I'm a standup guy and can be trusted with my band to practice here?"

Stacy laughed. "He's a standup guy and can be trusted. Seriously though, you don't have to worry where Bryan in concerned." She winked at him and went back to bussing the tables.

Confusion filled Annika's eyes. "How do we know each other?"

"We both volunteered at Second Chance Animal shelter one summer. We weren't friends or anything, but—"

"Oh!" Recognition crossed her face. "I remember you now. Sorry, that time seems like so long ago, and you've changed since you were thirteen or fourteen."

"Thank the Lord for that. I'd hate to be that awkward still. So what do you say? Can my band practice here?"

She pressed her lips together and stared at the brick wall.

Maybe the rumor he'd heard about Amanda was true. He needed to make this worth her while if she really did dislike music. "Maybe we can work out a trade. If you will let us practice here two or three nights a week from seven to eight I will—"

She turned back to him and her face brightened. "Mop."

"Come again?"

"If I let your band practice here three nights a week, when you're finished I want one of you to mop the floors. I hate mopping." She brushed at an imaginary crumb. "Take it or leave it. Oh, and I can change my mind at any time."

"You're really going to let us practice here?"

"As it turns out, I'm looking for a band to play at Second Chance Animal Shelter's Christmas-in-July BBQ fundraiser. You might be an answer to prayer. That is if you're willing to play for food, and I like your sound."

"I happen to be a fan of animals and that shelter in particular, but I'll have to check with the guys before I commit to the gig. You have a deal on the practice space though." He thrust out his hand. "By the way, my name is Bryan Grant, in case you couldn't remember."

"I remember now. And I'm Annika Cooke."

He'd never forgotten her name. "I'll be in touch, but if you need to reach me before then, I'm a firefighter at Station One." He would hate for the guys to cart their equipment over here only to find out she had changed her mind.

"I didn't know there was more than one firehouse in town."

He chuckled. "There isn't. Our battalion has a crew of three plus the chief. We rely on a volunteer crew for when we need the ladder truck. I guess the name was a planning thing for the day when the town grows large enough to need more."

"Interesting. I hope I never have a need to call the fire department." She shivered and stood.

He took that as his cue to leave. "Thanks, and I'll get back to you soon about the charity event." He walked out with a little extra bounce in his step. Apparently the rumor around town that Annika didn't like music was wrong, especially since she so easily allowed his band practice space.

* * *

Annika followed her last customers to the door then flipped the lock and slid the sign to Closed. "What a day.

As soon as you load the dishwasher, Stacy, feel free to head out."

"Thanks." Stacy paused. "I couldn't help overhearing your conversation with Bryan, and I'm shocked that you would allow his band to play here."

"Why? Are they bad?" She'd had such high hopes for the handsome firefighter's band. Not having to interview a bunch of bands for the BBQ in July was the main reason she'd said yes to his request. Plus she'd kind of thought he was cute as a teen. Not that she'd ever admit that to him. She was surprised he even noticed her, considering how shy she'd been back then.

"I've never heard them, but according to one of their wives, they're good. I thought you hated musicians."

Annika's stomach lurched. "I never said that." She'd never marry a musician, thanks to her mother, but she didn't hate them. She was a musician herself. A closet one, but she'd been playing the piano and singing most of her life.

"I suppose I assumed that since your aunt always suspended Open Mic Night, when you visited. She said your mom was a musician and that she thought it would make you too homesick, but I had a feeling there was more to it than that."

"Really?" She loved her Aunt Annette and missed her terribly, but she'd had no idea just how thoughtful she had been to her feelings. "My mom is a musician, but I don't know how that would have made me feel. Maybe I would have been homesick. It's hard to say." She flipped another chair onto a tabletop. "Does the whole town think I dislike musicians?"

"Maybe." Stacy gave her a sheepish look.

Annika's shoulder's tensed. "Why would they think that?"

"I may have mentioned it when I spread the word there would no longer be an Open Mic Night here."

"Oh, so *that's* why the back door has been egged a few times!" No wonder Roxanne Mayberry, the co-owner of Second Chance Animal Shelter, had asked her to head up the musical entertainment for the shelter's fundraiser. She was trying to improve her image with the town's residents. That woman had been looking out for her since she was a young teen and apparently hadn't stopped now that she was an adult and plenty capable of taking care of herself.

A gentle touch on her shoulder drew her from her thoughts. Concern clouded Stacy's eyes. "I'm sorry for overstepping. I should have told you about Open Mic Night. It wasn't fair of me to assume you'd want to discontinue it when you didn't even know it existed."

"Until this evening that is, when Bryan mentioned it."

Stacy sucked in a breath. "I really messed up, didn't I?"

Annika nodded her head. "Yes, but it's fine. Really. Although I wish you'd talked to me before you drew conclusions about my position. I'm really not sure if I want to bring that tradition back or not. I'd like to make

Main Street Java my own without alienating my customer base."

"So you and I are okay?"

"Of course, Stacy. Without you showing me the ropes, I don't know how I would have managed. Those two summers I worked here were not enough to teach me how to run this place." She'd inherited Stacy as an employee from her aunt. She couldn't complain though. The happy-go-lucky blonde seemed acquainted with everyone and did her job well.

"Whew. Thanks." Stacy walked to the kitchen with a little extra bounce in her step. "Oh, if you decide to resurrect Open Mic Night, you might want to know I'm storing the sound equipment in my attic."

"You took equipment that belonged to my aunt?" Confusion whirled in her mind. Had she misplaced her trust in Stacy?

Stacy's face reddened. "I was only thinking of you. I didn't steal it. I was holding onto it for safe keeping."

Annika waved her hand. "I understand. You just surprised me. Why don't you bring it back though? Bryan's band may want to use it."

Stacy beamed a smile. "Will do."

It looked like allowing Bryan's band to rehearse here would be the first step in mending her reputation with the music lovers of Mistletoe Springs. Truth told she didn't hate musicians or music, but rather what that industry did to her growing up years.

She quickly ran a dry mop across the tiled floor with

a hardwood like finish. Her nightly ritual of mopping the floors had gotten old fast, and she looked forward to having the burden removed a few nights a week. Yes, this band thing could work out nicely for all of them.

"I'm headed out, Annika. See you Monday."

"Right. See you then."

She finished her closing ritual in about an hour then climbed the stairs to her second story apartment. Her feet screamed with every step. When would she get used to standing for eleven hours a day?

Business had been sluggish, but she had confidence things would pick up soon—failure was not an option. She owed it to Aunt Annette to make the business a success once again.

She clicked on the stove, then placed a pan with a little cooking oil on it to heat. She'd set a pork chop in the fridge to thaw yesterday. Her mouth watered just thinking about the savory meal.

Her thoughts drifted to Bryan and his band. Not that she was looking for a guy, but it really was too bad that Bryan was a musician. He was tall, dark, and handsome with a cute dimple in his right cheek, and he clearly worked out. Plus he was a fire fighter, and fine enough to grace the cover of any charity calendar. Too bad they weren't making a calendar and selling it to raise funds for the shelter, because no woman in town would be able to resist one filled with local hunks and adorable animals.

She flicked on the faucet and washed her hands. A crashing sound in the alley below drew her attention.

"What now?" She tossed the towel onto the counter then pulled the curtain aside and gazed down. Several teens slammed eggs against the shop's door below. She pushed the window up. "Hey!" She pulled her phone from her pocket and quickly snapped off several pictures as they ran away.

Maybe Stacy would recognize the kids. She hated to involve the police, but she would if this vandalism didn't stop soon. Rather than waste time scrubbing dried-on egg in the morning, she slipped on flip-flops and headed down to the coffee shop.

After filling a bucket with warm sudsy water, she tugged on dishwashing gloves and plodded into the alley. Five minutes later she stood back to inspect her work.

"Everything okay?"

She whirled around and spotted Bryan at the end of the alley. Her heart hammered in her chest. "You startled me. What are you doing here?"

"Walking Rusty."

She glanced down at the black dog by the side of his leg. "He's beautiful."

"Thanks." He sauntered toward her. "I saw some kids running down the street. Would they happen to have anything to do with this?"

"Probably," she said drily. "A few teens seem to think my door needs to be christened with eggs on a semi-daily basis."

A frown marred his face. "Do you have security cameras back here?"

"No. But that's a good idea." She tugged the gloves off and pulled her cell phone from her pocket. "I managed to snap a few photos as they were running away." She pulled up the pictures and handed the phone to him.

"Hmm. I think I know one of them. Any idea why they're targeting your business?"

"No clue, but they must have lots of money to waste. Eggs aren't cheap."

"Unless they have their own chickens."

"Good point."

"Are you having any other trouble?"

"No." And she hoped it stayed that way. She had enough to deal with already.

He pulled a card from his wallet. "Give me a call if you need anything."

She took the card. "Thanks, but I don't think that will be necessary. It's just a few kids and a harmless prank."

"I understand, but you never know." Bryan's dog plopped down and rested his head on his front paws. "This is a lousy way to be welcomed back to town."

"Agreed." She should probably head inside, but Bryan's friendliness was balm to her frayed nerves.

"As I recall, you always had your nose in a book when you were younger."

She chuckled. "That sounds like me." Her summertime friends for the most part had been the animals at the shelter and the characters in the books she'd read. It was enough at the time, but she now regretted not getting to know more people here when she was a kid. It would have made this transition so much smoother. "I still enjoy reading, but now when I close up I'm too tired. If I sit for more than a few minutes I'm sure I'd fall asleep."

He chuckled. "I hear that."

An alarm blared into the quiet evening.

"That sounds like it's coming from inside your place."

Her heart skidded, then hammered in her chest. "I left the stove on." She looked up at the window. "There's smoke!" What had she done?

"Call 911. Rusty, stay." He yanked the door open and charged into the building.

# 2

Bryan ran to the end of the hall toward the coffee shop's kitchen. Everything looked fine there. He grabbed the fire extinguisher off the wall and charged up the stairs to the apartment above. He twisted the doorknob and went inside.

Flames licked at the hood above the stove. He pulled the pin from the extinguisher and doused the fire until all the flames were out. He opened a second window across the room from the one already open, then fanned the smoke detector until it stopped blaring. Too bad it hadn't been closer to the kitchen. They may have been able to catch the problem before it did any damage.

A cross-breeze helped to air the space. Maybe the place would clear before the smoke caused further damage. A siren wailed, and he trotted down the stairs and through the door into the alley.

"How bad?" Annika asked with a note of panic in her voice.

"It could have been much worse." He guided her

gently away from the building, noting her pale face. "Are you okay?"

She nodded but didn't look any better.

He tugged her toward the sidewalk where the engine truck had pulled to a stop. He approached Captain Jamison as he bounded from the truck.

"The fire is out and was isolated to the stove. We just need to check for extension." Standard procedure dictated they check to make sure there was no fire in the walls where the flames had licked. The fire hadn't been bad, so he suspected there would be no extension.

"Good to hear. I'll grab the T.I.C."

Bryan waited for him to get the thermal imaging camera and turned to Annika. "Would you mind keeping Rusty out here with you?"

"You're positive the fire is out?"

"As positive as I can be without tearing into the walls."

She bit down on her bottom lip then raised her chin. "Rusty can come in with us. I want to see the damage."

Bryan nodded and led the way up the stairs. "Like I said, the fire was contained to the stove. It looks like it started as a grease fire then spread to that charred hand towel."

"Since the damage isn't too bad, I don't want to tear into the wall." Captain Jamison aimed the T.I.C. at the wall behind the stove and adjacent counter. "Looks good. You were lucky."

"I guess so." Annika's voice caught and she cleared

her throat. "I owe you, Bryan. Thanks."

"Right place, right time. Anyone would have done the same thing."

"I don't know about that. Not everyone in this town likes me. Besides, I never would have charged up here like you did. I would have been too afraid. "

Captain Jamison nodded to them. "I'll see myself out."

"Thank you," Annika called after him.

She swayed slightly. He reached out to steady her. "You really are afraid of fire. Come sit for a few minutes." He kept a steadying hand on her elbow as she went downstairs to the coffee shop.

Annika sank onto the nearest chair and closed her eyes. Rusty nuzzled against her legs. "You're a sweet dog." She scratched his back with a shaky hand.

Bryan sat in the chair across from her. "I should probably tie Rusty up outside." He patted his thigh.

"Your dog is fine. I know he's not supposed to be in here, but I don't care right now. I love animals, especially dogs." She continued to rub her hand along Rusty's back seeming lost in the motion. "Just don't rat me out to the health inspector."

"I promise." Rusty's calming effect on Annika didn't surprise him. Dogs had a way of comforting people. She focused on his dog. "I've been terrified of fire most of my life." She looked up and met his eyes. "It's kind of funny that when you see a fire you run toward it, and when I see or even think there might be one, I go the opposite direction."

"Life experiences mold how we respond to things." He rested his elbows on the table between them. "If you don't mind sharing, what happened to make you so afraid of fire?"

She traced a finger along the tabletop, then paused. "When I was five, I woke up to smoke in my bedroom. We had just talked about fire safety in my kindergarten class, so I climbed out of bed and crawled to the door. The handle was hot." Her gaze lost its focus. "I could feel the heat on the other side of the door, and I was terrified. I started screaming for my mom and dad."

He swallowed the lump in his throat almost afraid to hear the rest of her story. If the haunted look in her eyes was any indication, her story wouldn't end well.

"The smoke kept getting worse and no one came for me. I crawled to my window and tried to open it, but it wouldn't budge."

"What happened?" His voice was barely above a whisper.

"I passed out from the smoke and woke up in the hospital. My mom told me a fireman rescued me. My bedroom was upstairs and Mom and Dad slept downstairs. An electrical short in an upstairs wall caused the fire. It was fully engaged before they even knew what was happening." Her haunted eyes sought out his. "Dad ran though the fire to get to me. He didn't make it."

He reached across the table and placed his fingers over her freezing hand and gave it a gentle squeeze. "I'm so sorry."

They sat in silence for several minutes. She finally shifted and spoke with conviction. "I make sure there are always working smoke detectors wherever I am living."

"I take it there were no working smoke detectors that night."

She shook her head. "If there had been, my dad would still be alive, and my life would have been very different."

Given his profession, he'd seen and felt loss, but no words of comfort would come. "Are you and your mom close?"

She slid her hand from his. "Why would you ask that?"

His stomach knotted. "I don't know. It just popped into my head."

"My mom and I have a complicated relationship. That's why I spent my summers here as a kid. When I was old enough, I started volunteering at Second Chances Animal Shelter. I missed that place when I went home at the end of summer. I'm so glad it's still around, although I haven't had the time to volunteer since I've been trying to get this shop revamped." She shook her head. "I know one thing for sure. I will never be a firefighter." The color had returned to her cheeks, and her breathing was steady. "I need to talk about something else. Do you mind if I ask you an off topic question?"

"Go ahead." He had no intention of leaving her alone until she was out of shock. She appeared to be doing much better. The haunted look had finally cleared from her eyes and her tone was stronger.

"What did I do to make people here dislike me?"

He winced at the pain in her voice. "That came out of nowhere. What makes you think you're disliked?"

"The eggs on my door. The dirty looks from various people." She shrugged. "I don't know what I did. I'm a nice person."

"It really has nothing directly to do with you. Open Mic Night was a big deal. When it went away, a lot of people were not happy." He'd heard a few unkind things about the new owner of Main Street Java, but now that he'd become reacquainted with Annika, their words disturbed him. They did not define her at all.

"I didn't even know about Open Mic Night until today. How can they hold something against me when I was given no choice in the matter?"

"You didn't know?" He leaned forward resting his elbows on his knees.

"I'm afraid what my aunt intended for good has come back to bite me in the backside. Stacy even went so far as to remove all the sound equipment from the building so I wouldn't know about the tradition. I really don't blame her though. She thought she was doing the right thing, but now everyone is angry with me and business is sluggish. At this rate I won't make it to the end of the year."

"I'm sorry about all of this. I wish there was something I could do to make things easier for you."

Her cheeks flushed. "Thanks, and I'm sorry for dropping my problems on you. I didn't mean to have a pity party."

"Hey, I understand. Sometimes a person needs to vent. I'd say tonight you are entitled, so it's okay." He meant it too. Clearly Annika didn't walk an easy road, and most of the time she probably hid her pain. It felt good that she trusted him enough to share her burdens. "Do you have someplace where you can stay tonight while this place airs out? We both reek like smoke, as it is."

Silence.

"Annika," he said softly. "Who do you know in town?"

"Roxanne and Scott Mayberry and Stacy. But I can't ask them. The Mayberrys just found out they lost funding for their shelter, and I can't impose on them like that."

"Then Stacy."

"No. It's fine. I can stay down here. The smoke didn't reach the shop."

He frowned. Clearly she was stubborn, and arguing would do no good. "Okay. It's getting late and my shift at the fire station starts at eight tomorrow morning, so I need to head out, but if you need anything, please call me."

She stood and walked him to the door leading to the alley, then squatted to Rusty's level. "Goodbye, buddy. You're a good boy." She gave him a rub along his neck, then stood. "Be safe, Bryan."

"I'll try. Oh, I talked to the guys. Does Monday work

for our first practice?"

"Sure."

"Thanks. See you." Annika tugged at a place in his heart he had thought sealed off. "Come on, boy. Let's go home." He took off at a run. They'd never made it to the park, and Rusty needed to stretch his legs.

He was glad he'd happened by the alley this evening, or no telling what would have happened. One thing was certain, he'd make a point of stopping by here more often. Clearly Annika needed someone on her side and he wanted to be that someone.

\* \* \*

Monday afternoon, Annika pulled a box from a shelf and hefted it to the dining area of her coffee shop. With a box knife, she sliced through the packing tape and pulled up the lid. The aroma of coffee beans punched the air. "I will never get tired of that smell."

"Hey there, girl! I heard you were back."

Annika looked to the left. "Lisa!" She pulled her friend from long ago into a hug. "What are you doing here? I thought you were living in California." Her strawberry-blonde haired, green-eyed friend looked exactly the way she remembered.

"I moved home a few months ago."

"It's so good to see you." Annika couldn't stop grinning. Lisa was the exception to her lack of friends growing up. They'd met the summer of her junior year and had lost touch during college. "Do you have some time to visit? You can keep me company while I stock the coffee."

"Sure. Let me order a latte, and we'll catch up."

"I'll make us each one. Be back in a few." Annika hustled around the counter. "Do you still like vanilla lattes?"

Lisa nodded. "Great memory."

"We only came here every day of the summer. It wasn't *that* long ago." She quickly created two vanilla lattes then set them on the table beside the shelf she'd been stocking. "I'll have this done in no time." She wouldn't bother except that the order had arrived several days late and their coffee supply had dwindled to nearly nothing. Five minutes later, she tossed the box in the closet to recycle later then sat across from her friend.

Lisa took a sip from her cup. "This tastes exactly like I remember."

"Good. At least I'm doing something right."

"Oh, now that sounds like a story."

"Nothing worth talking about. What brought you back to town?"

"I was homesick," Lisa said. A shadow of wariness clouded her eyes for a moment then vanished.

"No way. You always talked about how you were going to college and would never come back." If anyone had a story to tell, it was Lisa.

"Yeah, well, life has a way of changing our best laid plans. Truth is, I got married and divorced in the past six months. The divorce did a number on me, and I came home to live with my parents until I can get back on my feet."

"I had no idea you got married. Why didn't you send me an invitation to the wedding?"

"We eloped. It was a whirlwind romance, and a huge mistake that cost me my small savings."

"Oh, wow. I'm so sorry. So what are you doing now?" Her friend never expressed a desire to get married, so a whirlwind romance felt out of character.

"I'm studying to get my real estate license and working part time for my mom as her assistant. She's a writer, and I do all her marketing."

"Cool. What does she write?" Excitement bubbled in her voice. She may not have much time for reading these days, but she'd never lost her love of books.

"Christian romance. She's an independent writer and puts out a new book every three to four months."

"Again, very cool." Christian romance was her favorite genre.

"Thanks. She has a few copies of her books on hand. I'll bring you some to read. I assume you still love reading."

"Of course, but I don't have much time anymore." Annika studied her friend. Although she had the same bobbed haircut and freckles, there was something different about Lisa. She seemed older, and not in a good way. "You know . . . I've been open less than a week, and I need to hire some new help since a few of the people my aunt employed quit. If you need another job in your already busy schedule, I have openings."

Lisa stilled. "I'd love that. Mom's job is very part time, and I could use the money. When can I start?"

Annika chuckled. "The pay is minimum wage to begin with, and you won't get more than twenty hours a week *and* there are no benefits. Still interested?"

"Yes." Her friend's green eyes sparkled for the first time since they'd sat down.

"Great! How about tomorrow, say, one o'clock? It's a little slower that time of day, and it would be a good time to train you and fill out paperwork."

"I'll be here. I need to run. See you tomorrow."

Annika gave Lisa a quick hug then got back to work. It was nice to finally have a friend in town. Not that she was incapable of making new friends, but working constantly made it difficult.

Her cell phone rang. She checked the caller ID and groaned. Her mom never called unless she wanted something and it was seldom good.

# 3

Annika motioned to Stacy that she was taking a call, then cradled the phone to her ear as she raced up the stairs to her apartment. "Hi, Mom." She closed the door and plopped onto the couch. She wanted to be seated in the privacy of her home before hearing whatever her mother had to dole out this time.

"Hi, yourself. How's it going in Mistletoe Springs?"

"Not bad. All the coffee shop updates are finished. I did a soft open, and I'm considering having a formal grand re-opening."

"What a wonderful idea. You should do it soon though, or you'll miss that window of opportunity, and people will wonder why you're having a grand re-opening when you've been in business for months."

"True. I've just been very busy."

Her mom ignored her comment and went on to list off everything Annika needed to do in preparation for the event. "And I want to be there. If you'd like entertainment, I'll bring my guitar along and do a few songs."

Having her mother perform in the shop might go a long way to mending a few opinions about her. Her mom was good. The only thing Annika resented was that Mom's career always came first and her family last. But in this case it was a win-win. "Performing here is a great idea, Mom. I'll get some fliers worked up, post an ad in the paper, and put it up on the shop's website. Send me your current promo picture, and I'll have it up before the end of the day."

"Wonderful! I'm sending the photo now. I'm really looking forward to this. The only thing is, I need it to be this weekend."

"What? I can't pull this together in four days!"

"Sure you can. There's not that much to do. Plus, I'd like to be there, but my summer tour starts early this year and this coming weekend is my only free time."

Annika frowned into the phone. Her mom could've brought this up sooner, so she'd have time to plan. But then again it wouldn't take long to get the word out and order several dozen cookies from the bakery. "Okay. Let's do this."

"Great! Love you."

"You too." She tucked the phone in her pocket and kicked her feet onto the coffee table. Never in her wildest imagination did she think her mom would volunteer to play at her shop. Mom had always been about herself when it came to her career. She rarely did charity events or Annika would have booked her for the shelter's fundraiser.

She hopped up and trotted down to the coffee shop. Stacy was behind the counter helping a customer, but otherwise the place was quiet, so she detoured to the kitchen and got busy on the flyer. An hour later she had the website updated, scheduled a week's worth of tweets and sent the flier document to the copy center for printing. The fliers would be ready by five. All that was left was to order the cookies.

With an extra bounce in her step, she waved to Stacy and promised to be back soon. She trotted across the street to the bakery and paused inside the doorway. Sweets 'n Treats had an exposed brick wall just like hers, but the color scheme was nothing like the coffee shop's. Where she'd chosen warm coffee-inspired colors, the bakery had a light and airy feel with a mint green and cream striped wall and white table and chairs set off to the right of the entrance. Overall, the effect was inviting.

Annika's clogs clicked on the hardwood floor as she walked straight ahead to a clear glass case filled with a variety of cookies—exactly what she was looking for.

"Hi there," she said to a brown-haired woman wearing a pretty mint-green-and-cream striped apron. "I'd like to order twelve dozen cookies, and I need them Saturday morning."

The woman's eyes widened. "Are you having a party?"

"A grand re-opening. I own Main Street Java." She held out her hand. "I'm Annika."

"Jamie. You must be Annette's niece. I remember seeing you at the shelter fundraiser meeting, but I didn't place you with Main Street Java." The younger woman shook her hand before grabbing a pen and pad of paper. "I'm sorry we haven't gotten to know each other, especially with our shops so close to one another."

Annika waved a hand. "I don't get out much. I've been so busy updating the shop and learning how things are done there that I've practically been a hermit."

"I imagine you will meet lots of people at your event." Jamie grinned.

"I hope so." She eyed the display case and her mouth watered. So many choices. "What do you recommend?"

"They're all customer favorites. I suggest an assortment."

"Great idea."

Jamie studied the cookies, head cocked to one side. "Then . . . chocolate chip for sure. How about if I make up four dozen each of oatmeal, white chocolate macadamia and chocolate chip. You're sure to cover most of your customers with that selection."

"Perfect. I hope you'll stop in on Saturday. Penelope Rush will be performing at noon."

"I've heard of her. How exciting to have a famous singer in Mistletoe Springs."

"Right." She had a difficult time matching the enthusiasm of many of the towns' residents, but worked at playing along. Penelope Rush might be her mother's stage name, but to Annika she was just Mom or her real name, Deloris Cooke. She looked forward to some mom and daughter time. In spite of everything, she loved her mom. Annika paid for her order and headed back to work.

* * *

The rest of the week flew by in a blur, and unlike most days, Friday's closing snuck up on her. All the preparations were in place for tomorrow's grand re-opening. Her mother would be flying in this evening. Annika couldn't wait. She felt like they'd finally turned a corner in their relationship, and her mom was actually trying to be a part of her life.

It was no secret, as a child she'd resented her mother's career, and the attitude had carried over into adulthood. Now that her mom had reached out and was sharing herself, Annika was trying to give her the benefit of the doubt and view her in a whole new light.

The buzz around town sizzled in anticipation of Penelope Rush performing at Main Street Java. The best part of all was that people in town were smiling at her and saying hello when they saw her. Talk about a switcheroo. Who would have thought bringing her mom to town would cause people to be nice to her?

The door swung open. She looked up to see who'd popped in right at closing time and grinned. Now this was a good way to end a day. "Hey there, Bryan. I forgot you and your band were practicing tonight. Stacy brought the sound equipment in and left it in the storage room." Her mom would set up whatever she needed in the morning.

"I think we can do without it tonight." He laid a guitar case on a table and asked the three other guys to move the tables away from the brick wall. "You don't mind, do you?" He cast her a quizzical glance.

"Of course not. In fact, there's no need to return the tables to their place since Penelope Rush will be setting up here in the morning." She worried her bottom lip. Mom should have been here an hour ago. She'd tried texting and then calling, but there was no response.

Annika observed the band as she went through her closing ritual. They all wore jeans and T-shirts and sort of reminded her of a boy-band with their put-together look, albeit these guys were grown men, not teens.

Would giving up the stage space so the guys wouldn't have to move things around every time they practiced hurt business? She could shift the layout easily enough and maybe only lose one or two tables. She'd have to experiment with the tables to know for sure, but it would be nice to save them the set up time. The sooner they finished practicing the sooner she could call it a night.

Her cell rang. *Mom.* "Hey. Where are you?"

"Honey, I can barely hear you."

"Sorry." She moved to the kitchen and closed the door. "Better?"

"Much. I've been busy and just saw your texts and that you called. I'm so sorry, but I'm not going to make it for the grand re-opening."

"What?" Annika took a calming breath. "Why won't you be here? Are you okay?"

"I'm fine. It's just that there is so much to do before I leave for tour. Honestly, I completely forgot and didn't even book a flight."

"You said you would be flying in tonight." This couldn't be happening! Mom had never been the greatest parent, but she was always professional.

"I did? Hmm, well, nonetheless I won't be there."

"I've been promoting you all week just like you suggested. Mom, you can't do this. There's still time for you to get a flight and be here for the concert."

"I wish I could, but I'll make it up to you. I have to go now. Love you."

Annika's entire body shook. Angry tears spilled down her face. She swiped them away and thrust her phone into her pocket. That was it! Never again! She was done with her mother and anything that reminded her of Penelope Rush. She'd do the thing for the shelter, but that was it. No Open Mic Night. No band practices. Nothing.

Music blared from the dining area. She rammed her hands over her ears and squeezed. The sound muffled. "This is useless." Maybe if she kept busy she could block out the sound from her mind. She pulled on rubber gloves and grabbed a scouring pad. Back and forth she ran the scrubber over the sink.

"You're going to wear a hole in that sink if you keep scrubbing like that."

She gasped and whirled around. "Bryan. I didn't hear you come in."

"Sorry. I didn't mean to startle you. Is something bothering you?"

"Nope." *Yes!*

He tilted his head. "Okay. If you say so, but the only time my mom scrubs like that is when she is upset. Have you had any more problems with those teens?"

She shook her head and tossed the worn out scouring pad into the garbage.

"Good. You'll let me know though if they egg your door again?"

"Why?" She titled her head.

"Thought I'd save you the work of scrubbing your door. I'll spray it with the fire hose." He winked. "Seriously though, the band is finished, and I came for the mop and bucket."

"You don't have to ask to get it." She yanked off her gloves and strode into the cleaning closet. The mop sat exactly where she'd left it the day before. She pulled it out and turned, bumping into Bryan. Her skin tingled at his closeness. She hopped back.

"Sorry."

"It's okay." She thrust the mop into his hand, then rushed into the dining room stopping at the counter. She needed to get it together.

Bryan rolled the bucket to the far corner and pushed the mop back and forth in a steady rhythm. "So I talked to the guys and they're in, if you'd still like for us to play at the charity BBQ."

"You have a great sound, so yes, I would."

"It's a Christmas theme right?"

"Uh-huh." She bit her bottom lip. "Bryan, I need to tell you something, and you're not going to like it."

He stopped mopping and stood facing her. "Okay." He drew the word out.

"Your band can't practice here anymore."

His head jerked back as if he'd been struck.

She rushed on. "I thought I could handle having the band here, but I can't. It's too hard."

"It's too hard?" He put the mop in the bucket and marched over to her side. Crossing his arms, he leaned onto the counter. "I know we're not the best band around, but since you want us to perform at the fundraiser, I have to assume you like our group. So, why can't we practice here?"

Annika took a deep breath and let it out slowly. She hated confrontation. "I can't explain why."

"Come on. You at least owe me that." Irritation laced his voice.

She shook her head and stepped away from the counter "I'll finish mopping. You can go." She strode across the room, and her foot came out from under her. She waved her arms and grasped at the air. Her body hit the floor and air whooshed from her lungs as her head smacked the tile.

# 4

Bryan cradled Annika's cheek in the palm of his hand. "Stay with me, Annika. Slow, deep breaths." He had tried to reach her before she'd fallen, but had nearly fallen on the wet floor himself. Next time he'd squeeze the mop out better, if there was a next time.

Her eyelids fluttered as she took a shaky breath, then another.

"That's it. Nice and easy."

Annika tried to sit up.

"Go slow. I don't want you passing out again."

"I'm okay. I think I only knocked the wind out of me."

"You hit your head pretty hard and appeared to be unconscious for a few seconds."

She rubbed the back of her head and grimaced. "No. I just couldn't catch my breath. I'll be fine."

"I'd feel better if you went to the hospital and got checked out."

"I'm okay. Really." She sat up and stood with little

effort. "See?"

Maybe she was right, but he'd seen too many people think they were fine after a head injury only to discover later they were anything but. "I'm not taking no for an answer. My truck is out front. I'm taking you to the hospital. I don't want to show up for the grand re-opening tomorrow and find you dead in your apartment."

She gasped. "I'm not going to die from a simple fall."

"You hit your head." She clearly didn't understand the risk she was taking with her health, or she'd be one step ahead of him on the way to his pickup. "Look, I don't mean to upset you, but I'm concerned." He held out his hand. "Please, Annika? I won't sleep unless I know you're okay." Call it an occupational hazard, but he meant every word. He'd seen too much, knew too much and didn't want anything bad to happen to Annika.

She crossed her arms. "Fine." She marched to the door. "I appreciate your concern, but you will feel silly when you find out there's nothing wrong with me, other than a little bump." She rubbed the back of her head and winced.

Not half as silly as she looked having a mild tantrum about going to the hospital. He held back a grin. The lady had spunk; he'd give her that. "My motto is better safe than sorry." He didn't blame her for not wanting to go to the hospital, but it was the prudent thing to do.

With a sigh, she pushed open the door then locked up after him. "I hope the Emergency Department isn't too busy. I have a lot to do to get ready for tomorrow."

He held the passenger side door open and waited for her to hop in. "When's Penelope Rush getting here?" Maybe if he changed the subject she'd relax.

Her face darkened, and she pressed her lips together.

Oh boy, bad choice of topic. He pulled away from the curb. "I'm not really a fan, but I've heard of her."

"You should listen to her stuff sometime. She has a nice sound, but you'll have to download a song because she's not going to be performing tomorrow."

He shot a glance her way. "I'm sorry to hear that. What are you going to do?"

"I don't know. I guess I'll make an announcement on my website that she cancelled."

"I'm sorry your entertainment didn't work out, but I hope she at least refunds your deposit." He'd offer his own band, but they weren't ready.

Silence.

He pulled into the Emergency Department's parking lot and walked beside Annika until they reached the check-in desk. "I'll be waiting over there." He pointed to a series of plastic-looking chairs connected together in sets of six.

He eased down onto one of the uncomfortable looking seats and kept an eye on Annika. Clearly something had happened this evening to upset her. Could it be Penelope's cancellation or was it something else? Had one of the guys in the band said or done something?

Whatever it was, it was big enough to get her to kick them out of their practice space. What would they do now? They needed a place to practice if they were going to perform at the fundraising event. Plus the guys wanted to start playing gigs on a regular basis. They couldn't do that if they didn't practice.

Annika plopped beside him and crossed one leg over the other. "It shouldn't be long."

"Good."

"You don't have to wait." She shot him a look that clearly said she wanted him to leave.

Too bad. "Yes, I do. I brought you here, and I'm not leaving without you."

Her hand shot to her face, and she swiped at it. Was she crying? He looked more closely at her profile, and his gut clenched. Had he caused those tears? "Annika, look—"

"Annika," a nurse wearing scrubs called.

Annika rocketed from her seat. "Right here." Without looking back, she disappeared behind secure doors.

His pager went off. Torn between waiting for Annika and responding to the emergency his pager indicated, he did the only thing he could. He stood and moved to the reception desk. "Excuse me."

The receptionist looked up from her computer. "My friend, Annika Cooke, just went in there. I was supposed to wait for her, but I'm on call tonight for the fire department."

"Say no more."

"Thanks!" He bolted from the hospital and raced for

the station. He'd been on call many times, but this was the first time his pager had gone off. Something big must have happened if they needed more than the regular battalion and volunteer crew.

* * *

Annika stood and shook the Emergency Department doctor's hand. "Thank you." The tall man looked to be just out of med school, but he appeared to know his stuff.

"Be careful, Annika. Although your tests came back negative for any problems, and you don't appear to have a concussion, that goose egg on the back of your head is going to be tender. No more falling and hitting your head, and take it easy.."

"I'll do my best. Hopefully you'll never see me in here again."

He nodded and left the room with a grin on his face. He probably thought she was a klutz. The nurse showed her out to the waiting room that was buzzing with activity. What had happened in such a short amount of time? She'd only been gone an hour. A quick scan of the faces in the room caused her stomach to sink. Where was Bryan? Had her temper sent him away after all? Remorse for the way she'd treated him ate at her. He was only being cautious and caring. She needed someone like him in her life on a permanent basis.

She couldn't deny the pull she felt toward him, but it would never work. Not with him being a firefighter.

Nothing against his profession, but she'd be beside herself with worry every time he went to work. She pressed her lips tight and pushed her wayward thoughts aside.

Bryan wouldn't leave her here, would he? She couldn't believe he would do that. It didn't seem like something he would do. Maybe he'd stepped into the restroom. She sat in the seat nearest the restrooms and waited. And waited.

A woman wearing a skirt and blouse with a hospital badge hanging from her neck approached. "Are you Annika Cooke?"

Annika stood. "Yes."

"Your friend asked me to tell you he had to leave on an emergency call."

"Oh. That's odd. I thought he was off duty."

"I don't know, but he had a pager."

"Any idea what happened?"

"No. Sorry."

"Okay. Thanks." She hustled from the waiting room then pulled out her cell. Maybe Lisa would be able to give her a ride home.

No answer. It looked like she'd be hoofing it. No matter. It wasn't really that far. Sliding doors whooshed open, and she stepped outside. The sun had set, and the streetlights shone bright. She shivered and rubbed her hands up and down her arms.

A horn tooted and a pickup pulled alongside her. "Want a ride?"

She did a double take. "Bryan? I thought you were out on a call."

"False alarm. Some new guy punched in the wrong number. I went rushing over there with lights ablaze, and all the guys were sitting around the television. They looked at me like I'd grown a second head."

Annika pulled the door open and slid inside. Warmth wrapped its comforting arms around her. "I'm glad there wasn't an emergency. I don't know how you do what you do." Or how the families of the firefighters handled the knowledge their spouse or child walked into burning buildings chancing fate. She shivered. She could never marry a man who put himself in danger like that.

"Cold?" He reached toward the heater.

"Not anymore. It feels nice in here. Thanks for coming back."

"You're welcome. I wasn't sure if I'd catch you or not, but I'm glad I did."

"Me too."

"I need to stop by my place and pick up Rusty. Do you mind? He's been locked indoors all evening."

"Of course not."

"Thanks. Do you need any extra help tomorrow with your grand re-opening?"

"I don't think so. I hired an old friend this week, so between Lisa, Stacy and me we should be okay. I imagine once people hear there won't be entertainment they may not come anyway."

"Sure they will. You're giving away free cookies and

half-price coffee. People love that."

She chuckled and winced. Her head had begun to pound. The doctor had warned her that might happen.

"I take it since you were released that all is well with your noggin?"

In spite of her headache, sore head, and utter emotional exhaustion she couldn't help but smile at his words. "No concussion. The doctor thinks I may have just had the wind knocked out of me, since none of the tests showed a brain trauma."

"Hmm. I'm surprised, but head injuries are weird." He pulled up to a bungalow and hopped out, leaving the engine running. "Be right back."

A few minutes later, Rusty bounded out the front door and catapulted into the cab of Bryan's pickup. The dog licked her face then settled between them, resting his paws on her legs.

"Hey, boy." She rubbed the fur behind his ears and laughed when he leaned into her hand.

"He loves that." Bryan pulled away from the house. "My dog will be your best friend if you keep that up."

"I could use a best friend, Rusty, and you're perfect." She continued to rub the spot behind his ear, and then moved to the other one.

Bryan stopped in front of the coffee shop. "Would you like me to walk you in and help clean up the mop and stuff?"

It was on the tip of her tongue to say no, but "I'd love that" came out instead. Maybe the doctor had been wrong, and the fall had affected her. The last thing she wanted was for him to come inside, but she'd already opened her mouth. She led the way inside and caught her breath. "Oh my. What happened here?"

# 5

"Surprise!" Lisa and Stacy stood up from behind the counter.

Annika covered her mouth with her hands. Her shop had been transformed from nice to special. "This is . . ." Words escaped her, and instead, the waterworks started.

"None of that nonsense," Stacy said.

Lisa rushed to her side and gave her a hug. "Bryan called Stacy, who called me, and we decided after what happened, you could use some help. I know it's not much, since we didn't have a lot of time, but I think it looks nice."

Annika pulled out of her long-time friend's embrace and looked around the coffee shop. All the tables had the special floral center pieces she'd planned to put out tonight after the band left, a huge banner that said "Grand Re-Opening" hung across the middle of the space, and the stage was put together. "It's perfect. You both did a great job." She motioned toward the stage with her hand. "We won't need that though. I'm sorry to be the bearer of bad news, but my mom bailed on me. Penelope Rush will not be performing."

"Your mom?" Surprise colored Bryan's tone.

She turned to him. "Yes, my mom is the famous or maybe not-so-famous Penelope Rush. Her real name is Deloris Cooke, but she thought that was too boring."

Lisa nodded. "She was right. Deloris Cooke lacks wow factor. And Bryan told us she's not coming, but Stacy had a brilliant idea." Lisa looked to Stacy.

"At least I hope you think it's brilliant. Remember the Open Mic Night tradition?"

Annika's stomach knotted. "Yes." She drew the word out slowly.

"I thought since we can't deliver the entertainment promised, we could revive the tradition for one evening. Your customers will love it, and I think it will go a long way in changing some attitudes toward you. Lisa and I agreed that we want to stay late and help you with the entertainment. Believe me, you'll need the help."

It was on the tip of her tongue to say *no way*, but logic reigned. This was a business, and it made sense. Letting the community perform in whatever medium they chose for one evening was a good idea. "Okay. Let's do this, girls. Tomorrow is going to feel like a marathon, so head home and rest. I'd like you both here at seven."

Lisa moaned. "You know I'm not a morning person."

Stacy frowned. "I thought we were staying closed until the ribbon cutting at nine."

"True, but there are last minute things that will need to be done."

Stacy's face brightened "What if Lisa is here by eight? That would still give us plenty of time to make sure everything is perfect."

"I see your point. But don't be late. I have to pick up the cookies from the bakery, and Stacy shouldn't have to do everything alone."

"Promise."

She hugged her friends then paused. This was the first time she'd thought of Stacy as a friend, but the woman really had become one. Only a true friend would have come out in the middle of the night to surprise her. "Thank you for this." She motioned a hand at the decorations.

"We were happy to step up. How's your head?"

"I have a headache, but the doctor said that was to be expected."

"No nausea? My friend smacked her head once and vomited for hours." Stacy wrinkled her nose.

"Gross. Thanks for sharing, but I'm fine."

"Then our work here is done. Let's go, Lisa. Morning will be here before we know it."

Her friends waved on their way out.

Annika turned to Bryan who'd been silently watching their exchange. "Thanks for calling in the troops."

"You're welcome. See you tomorrow."

"Okay." She followed him to the door and turned the lock with her key. Before hitting the lights, she placed a small sign on the door window about their altered hours for the big day. Hopefully her regulars wouldn't hold opening three hours late against her.

She rubbed her hands together, taking one more look around the room. Tomorrow was the big day. The day she would learn what the people here *really* thought of her.

\* \* \*

Pounding on her door dragged Annika from a sweet dream. She lugged herself from bed and yanked the door wide. "Stacy. What are you doing here so early?"

"Sweetie, it's after eight."

Annika's heart thudded. "Oh, no." Her hand shot to her hair. "I'm a mess. I'll be down in twenty minutes. Is Lisa here?"

"Yes."

"Good. Send her to Sweets 'n Treats to pick up the cookies."

"Will do. Is there anything else you need?"

She squeezed her eyes shut trying to calm her racing mind, so she could think. No use. "I don't know. I'll hurry." Good thing she'd set aside her outfit a few days ago. She'd chosen a flowing skirt along with a purple sweater. She'd complete the outfit with ankle boots. She rushed though her shower, then finger combed her hair and gently pulled it into a loose ponytail at the base of her neck. Her head was still too tender for a tight ponytail.

She quickly applied lip gloss and mascara, then dashed down to the shop. All was quiet save for the racket in the kitchen. What *was* that awful noise? It sounded like an animal in pain. She pushed into the kitchen and pulled up short.

Stacy stood frosting cinnamon rolls and singing at the top of her lungs.

"A-hem!"

Stacy jumped and whirled around. "You about knocked ten years off my life."

"Sorry. I didn't mean to sneak up on you."

"No worries. I had Lisa set up a small table with an assortment of the cookies. One of us can keep an eye on it and add to the supply as needed."

"Great idea. That will keep the kids and the kids at heart from taking too many at once. What's up with the cinnamon rolls? I don't have those on the menu board for today." As much as she appreciated Stacy's initiative she didn't want extra stuff to deal with.

"These aren't for the customers. They are for us. I prepared them at home and baked them here this morning. I thought the scent would mingle nicely with the coffee."

Annika's mouth watered. "You are officially my favorite person on the planet at the moment. I'm starving!"

Stacy laughed. "Here you go. Coffee is brewed and the ribbon cutting is in ten minutes. Sit. Eat, and try to relax. It may be your only chance today."

Annika poured a mug of medium roast coffee and did as Stacy suggested. The cinnamon rolls nearly melted in her mouth. They needed to carry these in the shop at least once a week. She made a mental note to talk to Stacy about her rolls.

She savored every bite then rinsed the dishes and ran upstairs to brush her teeth. The dull roar of voices grabbed her attention. She glanced out the window and her pulse kicked into overdrive. There was a crowd! She took a calming breath, then scooted downstairs. "Are you ready, ladies?" She looked to Stacy and Lisa who stood behind the counter.

"Ready," they said in unison.

Annika slipped out the door and was greeted by the mayor.

"It's about time. We were beginning to wonder if this was really going to happen." She raised a perfectly plucked brow. "Especially considering no one has seen Penelope Rush or evidence that she is even here."

She should have put up a sign on the door as well as made a late night call to the paper, but as they say hindsight is 20/20. "There has been a change in entertainment."

The mayor's face reddened. She lowered her voice and barely moved her lips. "I'm not here for your silly grand re-opening. I'm here for Penelope Rush. This is inexcusable!"

"I agree." Annika turned her attention to the crowd of about thirty and waved an arm to get their attention.

"Thank you all for coming out this morning. I know my Aunt Annette would be so pleased. So without any further adieu, I welcome you all to the new and improved Main Street Java." She cut the ceremonial ribbon and stepped inside holding the door as the people filtered inside. "There are free cookies on the table to the right and drinks are half-price today. Enjoy!"

Bryan brushed past her and parked himself by her side. "Everything okay?"

"Yes. Go get whatever drink you want. Tell Lisa I said to comp you."

"That's not necessary."

"It's the least I can do, all things considered."

He dipped his chin. "Thanks. Join me if you can."

"I don't think that will be possible."

The line to order quickly snaked to the door. "It looks like I need to go help." She offered Bryan her best smile and dashed behind the counter to take over the register and put Stacy on making drinks. Stacy made exceptional espresso creations, and since Lisa was still learning, that made the most sense.

"When will Penelope Rush be performing?" a middle age woman asked.

"Penelope had to cancel at the last minute."

"Oh no! Is she sick?"

"She's fine." Just too busy for her daughter. "Penelope heads out on her summer tour very soon, and as it turned out, she couldn't fit us into her schedule."

"Well, that's rude," the woman said.

"I agree. But we have something fun planned for this evening. I'm reinstating Open Mic Night for this evening only."

The woman's face lit. "A lot of folks will appreciate that. I'll help spread the word. What time?"

"Seven to nine."

"Wonderful! I hope this place does well. I used to come here all the time when your aunt . . . I'm sorry. How are you holding up?"

Annika glanced nervously at the ever-growing line behind the friendly woman. "I'm okay. If you would step to that end of the counter, Lisa or Stacy will have your drink waiting."

The kind woman shot her a smile and moved away. Whew.

A scowling man stepped to the counter.

"Joe, right?"

He nodded. "I was here at my usual time and saw the sign on the door. Wish I'd known sooner."

"My apologies. This grand re-opening was rather sudden, and a few things were forgotten until the last minute. Can I make it up to you with a cup of coffee on the house?"

His lips pulled into a straight line. "That would help. Throw in one for my friend," he nodded to a woman sitting at a nearby table, "and I'll forget all about it."

She resisted rolling her eyes. "Done."

A few more regulars grumbled that they wish she'd told them she'd be opening late. Hopefully they wouldn't hold it against her. Annika needed this place to take off. She'd sunk all her savings into fixing it up, and if things didn't pick up soon, she didn't see how the place would stay open past the first six months.

She worked on autopilot for the next several hours until a commotion near the stage grabbed her attention. Now what? She rushed toward the stage.

# 6

Bryan stood outside Main Street Java holding his guitar case. Open Mic would start in a couple of hours, and he wanted to offer his assistance for the event. He looked through the plate-glass window and spotted Annika still working the register. Her head jerked to the right, and she frowned. *Hmm*. What was going on?

He pushed inside and stepped into the overly warm shop. Leaving the door open, he followed the direction of her gaze. A male teen held a microphone to his mouth and was beatboxing on the stage. The dude had potential. Then he started a less than kind rap aimed at Annika. His buddies at the foot of the stage whistled and clapped.

Bryan wove between occupied tables as he strode across the room and unplugged the microphone from the amp. "Not cool to disrespect the lady. Especially when she's having an Open Mic Night this evening."

The teen's eyes widened. "We didn't know about the open mic."

Annika sidled up to him. Her mouth pulled into a

frown. "I want all of you out of here. And if I find any more eggs on my door or walls or anyplace else, I'll send the authorities to hunt down the three of you."

The two who'd been encouraging the kid from the foot of the stage ran for the exit, knocking a kid down on the way. They didn't even stop to see if the little girl was okay. The beatboxer set the mic down and crossed his arms facing Annika. "How'd you know it was us?"

She pointed to his cap, then pulled her phone out and showed him the picture she'd taken.

He made an obscene gesture then skirted through the tables as he wove toward the exit.

A nearby patron gasped and stared directly at Annika. "I had hoped this place would be family friendly like it was when your aunt owned it, but if that social deviant is the kind of clientele that will be frequenting this place, I'll have my coffee elsewhere." She stood with a huff and left.

Bryan wanted to tell this woman off, but thought better of it. Instead he moved to go after the punk. "He can't get away with that." Annika's hand on his arm stopped him.

"Let him go." She sighed and released the hold on his arm. A mischievous grin covered her face. "What would you do to him anyway?"

His neck warmed. He hadn't thought that far ahead and shrugged. "Thanks for stopping me from doing something potentially stupid. You impressed me when you stood up to them." It was hard to believe this once reserved teen had grown into such a spunky woman. He liked her more now than ever. Even if she wouldn't let his band practice in her shop.

"Did I make a mistake? Do you think they'll do something worse now?"

"Hard to say, but they're aware you know who they are, so if anything happens, they'll get blamed. Not sure they're smart enough to put two and two together though."

"I hope they are. I don't want any more trouble. It's too bad he was a such jerk. I thought his beatboxing was pretty good."

"I'm surprised you even know what it is. You don't seem the type to get into that kind of thing."

"It's fascinating. I wish I could make those sounds with my mouth. Too bad it couldn't have turned out differently with them though. It would have been fun to have him back during Open Mic.

He motioned toward an empty table. "You have time for a break?"

She looked around the shop and shrugged. "I could use one, and it looks like things are slowing down. Did you eat? I could make us each a sandwich."

He knew her well enough to know if he said no, she wouldn't eat. "Sure."

"Turkey or ham?"

"How about both with a slice of white cheese and a smear of mustard."

She nodded. "I like a man who knows what he

wants. Be right back."

Placing his guitar case beside the table, he sat. Since he'd been here so much this past week, this place had begun to feel like a third home. The firehouse was his second. Too bad she'd kicked out his band. He still needed to break the news to the guys. He was hoping to change her mind on the grounds they needed a place to prepare their repertoire for the shelter's fundraiser.

Annika walked his way, balancing a plate and coffee mug in each hand. "Here we go. One Firefighter's Special and a black coffee." She slid the food his way and sat across from him.

"There's a Firefighter's Special? Why didn't I know that?"

"I just made it up." She smiled, bowed her head for a short moment, then she picked up her sandwich and took a huge bite, barely keeping her lips closed as she chewed. A twinkle lit her eyes.

He silently prayed a blessing over his food, a habit he'd let slide lately.

Annika set her sandwich on the plate. "The only thing that bothers me is that I didn't think of the ham and turkey combo first. This is good."

He chuckled before chomping into his sandwich. She was right; this was good, even if he would have preferred sourdough bread. "We could use you down at the firehouse sometime when it's my turn to cook." He waggled his brows.

Her brows drew together. "You don't cook?"

"I cook well enough, but I have a feeling the guys would enjoy this more than my specialty." He tilted his head. "They get a little sick of spaghetti and meat sauce."

"Mmm. That sounds delicious along with garlic bread and salad."

He waved to a buddy across the room. "Maybe the first couple of times, but it gets old fast. Trust me. You know . . . I've been thinking."

"Not that," she teased before taking another bite.

Her light-hearted mood surprised him considering the day she'd had, but he liked this side of Annika. It was nice to see her relaxed and playful. "Now that my band lost our practice space, I'm not sure we'll be able to do the shelter gig."

She frowned, pressing her lips tight.

Bryan washed the last bite down with his coffee. "Be right back." He wanted to give Annika a minute to think about what he'd said. He spied a small table with a tray of cookies and a sign that said complimentary. More than a little surprised that there were still free cookies available, he snagged one for each of them. By the time he sat back down, Annika looked more composed.

"Should I find a replacement for your band? By the way, what do you call yourselves?"

"We don't have a name. Yet."

"So this was your big break?"

"I guess. You want this cookie?"

"No, thanks." Good. He didn't feel like sharing, after all. One word described Annika Cooke—stubborn. Well, two could play that game. "I guess you'd better start interviewing bands. With no practice space we'll have to dissolve the group."

"Right. About that." She looked down at her lap then toward the stage and finally at him. "Tell you what. The days are getting longer, and it's not dark when I close the shop. How about if I walk Rusty while you and the band practice? I could use the exercise, and I imagine your dog would enjoy the attention."

He sat up straight. "He would. You trust us in here alone?"

"I trust *you*. That's enough." Without another word, she gathered their dishes and marched into the kitchen.

He couldn't figure Annika out. What did she have against listening to the band play? Clearly she liked their sound, or she'd have taken the out he'd offered. But, if it wasn't their sound, what was it? Before he could take his thoughts further, she strode toward him with a stack of papers and a large poster board.

"Do you have time to help spread the word about Open Mic Night? I wish I'd thought to have these ready to hang first thing this morning, but better late than never, I guess."

"Sure. I'll post it to Facebook and Twitter too. Can I stash my guitar here?"

"No problem. I need the poster mounted to the brick wall behind the stage." She pulled tape from her apron pocket. "Please put one of these up in the window and any other businesses that will allow you to."

"You got it. Be back soon." He felt like a schoolboy sent on a mission for someone special. Annika was worming her way into his thoughts and daily life far too much. He was done with dating, especially dating women who had a problem with him being a firefighter. Annika never said as much, but with her fear of fire, there was no way she'd ever be interested in him beyond friendship. He needed to get her out of his head.

\* \* \*

Annika rang up orders faster than either Stacy or Lisa could make them. Main Street Java was at capacity and people kept coming. What would she do? The roar in the shop gave her a headache, and the night was just starting. The clock said ten to seven. People leaned against walls and didn't even seem to mind there was no place to sit.

She handed Stacy the order, then turned to the next person in line. "Bryan. You're back. My goodness, you did a phenomenal job spreading the word about tonight. We are bursting at the seams."

"Yeah, about that. You can't let any more people in here. It's too hazardous, and against the law." He motioned toward the maximum occupancy sign on the wall.

She gasped. Bryan could shut her down with one phone call, but he was her friend. He wouldn't do that, but still . . . "How am I supposed to keep people out?" She looked at the sea of bodies and couldn't imagine one more person fitting in. Bryan was right. It was hazardous.

"Put a sign on the door that you're at capacity and no one else may enter."

"But that's impossible. People will come in anyway."

"No, they won't. I'll take care of it."

"You don't have to. It's my store, my job." She started to motion to Lisa to take over the register, but Bryan's words stopped her.

"Friends help each other. Who's emceeing?"

"I'd planned to, but I hadn't counted on being so busy."

"Let me call in reinforcements, then I'll emcee." He pulled his phone from his pocket, resting his gaze on her. "That is, if you don't mind."

"Please. I'd be crazy to turn down the help. Thanks!"

The crowd noise increased as seven o'clock neared. She needed to do something to calm everyone anxious for the entertainment to begin, and she knew of only one way to do that. She scanned the crowd for Bryan, but couldn't find him anywhere.

Here goes nothing. "Stacy, you're in charge."

"Huh? What's going on?"

Annika took off her apron then walked onto the stage where she'd placed her personal keyboard. Just because she had issues with her mother's music career didn't mean she wasn't a musician of sorts herself. After all, a person couldn't grow up in the same house with Penelope Rush and not have some musical ability.

She flipped the power switch to the microphone at

the keyboard. "Hi there." She kept her tone upbeat. "Thanks for coming out for Main Street Java's grand re-opening." The crowed hushed. "It's been quite a day and far exceeded my expectations. While we're waiting on the emcee, I thought I'd get us started with an old favorite. But before I do, I wanted to make you aware of Second Chance Shelter's event in July. The shelter recently lost its main source of funding and is hoping to raise the money to cover the difference. If you're interested in helping or purchasing tickets let me know." She looked at a conglomeration of familiar and unfamiliar faces and wondered what had possessed her to jump onto the stage. She hated public speaking. She cleared her suddenly dry throat. "To start us off, I'm going to sing a family favorite."

Looking down at the keyboard, she let instinct take over as the intro to one of her mother's original songs came to life. She hit a wrong note, but quickly recovered. What was she thinking? She'd never performed in public. She'd officially lost her mind. Maybe that bump on the head had affected her, after all.

She opened her mouth and sang the familiar words. Her voice wobbled. She could do this if she closed her eyes and pretended she was in her bedroom. Three minutes later, she opened her eyes and lifted her hands from the keyboard.

Shocked faces stared at her. Was it really that bad? Had her mother lied to her that she could sing?

Bryan hopped on the stage, microphone in hand.

"Let's give it up for Annika Cooke, owner of Main Street Java."

The room erupted in applause.

He whispered into her ear. "You've been holding out on us."

The rest of the evening went by in a blur. Several people introduced themselves and expressed interest in purchasing tickets for the Christmas in July fundraiser, and a few more offered to help.

Stacy and Lisa stood behind the service counter looking ready to drop. She owed them big time. "You can take off. Thanks for everything you did today."

"We can't leave now." Stacy said. "This place needs to be put back together."

"I'll get up early. Go home and rest."

Lisa untied her apron. "Thanks. I don't think I've ever been this tired. What a day."

"I agree." Annika sank into the nearest chair. "Never in my wildest imagination did I expect a turnout like this. Good thing I have a delivery on Monday. I'm about out of everything. Did you notice we ended up having a bouncer at the door?"

Stacy's eyes widened. "No. Why? How?"

"That was my doing," Bryan said as he came back from putting the sound equipment in the storage closet. "By the way, I promised Rick a hundred dollars."

"No problem." Annika stood. "He was worth every penny." She pulled five twenty-dollar bills from the till.

"That's not how you're supposed to do it." Stacy frowned. "There are proper ways to pay people."

"I'll record it in my books correctly. Now go home."

Stacy sighed. "Fine. Will you be okay here alone tomorrow?"

"Of course." But the first chance she had, she would advertise for more help. They would need another couple of baristas if business picked up, and she had confidence that after tonight, things would.

Annika followed her three life-savers to the door. "Thanks again, everyone. I could not have pulled this off without each of you."

Bryan waggled his brows. "Does this mean I'm off the hook for mopping?"

"In your dreams." Annika's insides flip-flopped as she laughed and gently pushed him out the door. She watched him saunter across the street and hop into his pickup. With a sigh she locked up and turned away, already missing his teasing grin.

Today had been over-the-top great. She quickly took the till to the safe and secured the days earnings. If the amount of bills stacked inside was any indication, they'd brought in more today than the entire week. Maybe her aunt's Open Mic Night was the key to making this business profitable. It was definitely something to consider.

Now if she could just get Bryan out of her head. Listening to him emcee all evening had done something to her heart, and she didn't like it, not one bit. She respected his profession, but couldn't allow herself to fall for a man who made a habit of running into burning buildings.

# 7

Monday morning, Bryan hosed off the engine truck. Keeping the equipment clean and in good working order was a top priority.

"Catch." Jim Morris tossed a rag his direction. "I heard your new girlfriend's grand re-opening was a huge success."

Bryan turned off the hose. "I thought I heard you say I have a girlfriend. News to me."

Jim laughed. "My mistake. So you and Annika aren't dating?"

"Nope."

"Mind if I ask her out?"

A flash of annoyance rushed through him. Why should it bother him if someone wanted to date Annika? She wasn't his. "Suit yourself, but she won't say yes." At least he hoped she would say no. Nothing against Jim, but the thought of another guy with Annika knotted his stomach.

Jim raised his chin. "Why's that?"

"She'll never date a firefighter. Her dad was killed in a house fire, and she's still traumatized whenever she even thinks there could be a fire." Bryan had known the minute Annika shared her story with him that there could never be anything more than friendship between them. Firefighting was in his DNA. His dad was a fireman and his dad's dad had been one too. The Grant men fought fires and had been doing so for over fifty years. Dad retired a few years ago, but it was obvious he missed the action.

Jim blew out a breath. "That's rough, but what makes you think that she won't date a firefighter?"

He wanted to say "duh," but held in the jab. "She's terrified of fire. Can you imagine what she'd be like every time she found out you were on a call?" Bryan shook his head. "She'd be a mess, and it's not fair to put her in that position."

"So you *do* have a thing for her."

"Give it a rest. Don't you have a hose to inspect?"

"Slave driver," Jim mumbled and walked away.

The alarm sounded. His adrenalin spiked as he tossed the dirty rag in the bin, then quickly pulled on his gear. He climbed behind the wheel. Jim sat behind him along with Greg, another firefighter. The captain sat up front. Less than a minute later they pulled out of the station. Siren blaring, they headed south on Sowell toward the high school. They stopped in front of the school. Captain Jamison hopped out first to assess the situation.

From all outward appearances, everything looked

fine. The students stood in the parking lot. A man wearing a suit, probably the principal, approached the Captain.

The principal stood at the front of the engine truck talking with their captain. His strong voice easily travelled. "There was a fire in the boys bathroom, but the janitor was able to put it out. Sorry to bring you all out here like this."

The Captain nodded. "We'll take a look and make sure all is clear then head out."

Twenty minutes later Bryan's stomach growled as he climbed into the truck. "Well, that was fun," he said drily. The fire had actually reignited, so it was a good thing they'd showed up. It was thoroughly out now.

"I hate calls to schools," Jim said.

"Me too. I'm just glad the fire was contained in the bathroom." Bryan started the engine.

"See you around." Captain Jamison shook the principal's hand then climbed into the front seat.

Bryan gazed out the window. The adrenaline buzz he got when the alarm sounded would gradually wear off, but right now he wanted to shoot hoops or take Rusty for a run in the park. Too bad his shift just started. "Hey, anyone mind stopping at Main Street Java?"

"Not me." The captain patted his stomach. "I missed breakfast and could use a snack." The captain cleared his throat. "I hear you're sweet on the new owner. That wouldn't happen to be why you want to stop, would it?"

"I'm not sweet on Annika. I'm hungry and need a

good cup of coffee. That swill Jim made this morning doesn't qualify."

"Hey! I happen to like the coffee I made."

"You drink it then," Bryan said.

"Stop your arguing, children," Captain Jamison chided as Bryan pulled to a stop. "We'll walk from here."

It was only a half block. "You coming, Jim? Greg?"

"No, I'll wait here," Jim said.

"A white chocolate mocha sounds good to me." The captain stepped down out of the truck, took off his gear, and left it in the truck.

Jim mumbled something about a frou-frou drink.

"Don't knock it until you try it, buddy." Bryan followed the captain's example and left his gear behind, then met him at the front of the truck. They strode at an easy pace toward Main Street Java.

"What's the deal with Jim today?" Bryan asked. "He's in a sour mood."

"He's pulling a double shift."

"Oh." Working a back-to-back twenty-four-hour shift would make *him* crabby too. He pushed into the shop and breathed in deeply the rich coffee aroma. "I love that smell." He spotted Annika as she stepped behind the counter. She wore jeans and a black T-shirt with her hair falling freely about her shoulders. Her gaze caught his, and she gave a little wave.

Captain Jamison patted him on the back. "Me too."

"You too what?"

"Love the smell of this place." He looked from

Annika to Bryan and grinned. "Hmm. Ever since her kitchen fire, I've been a regular."

Bryan raised a brow.

"I felt bad for her, so I came in the next day and got hooked on these things."

Bryan chuckled.

"Don't laugh. It's the best coffee in town." He walked up to the counter and slapped down a five-dollar bill. "I'll take my regular, Annika."

"Good to see you this morning, Rex." She sniffed the air. "Were you just on a call?"

"Small bathroom fire at the high school, but there's no reason for alarm."

She shivered. "I hate fire. I don't know how you guys do what you do, but I'm thankful nonetheless." She got busy at the espresso machine.

"I'm glad Bryan asked to stop by. I was running late earlier, so I couldn't get my normal cup of joe before my shift."

She smiled and handed him a large cup. "Enjoy. Glad you made it in."

Bryan stepped forward. "I'll try the same."

"Living dangerously, I see." A twinkle lit her eyes as if she had a secret she was dying to share.

"Always." Someone was in an especially good mood this morning. "How was the rest of your weekend?

"Blissfully quiet."

"No more trouble?"

"Nada."

"I'm glad." He didn't tell the guys, but he really chose to stop because he wanted to check on Annika. He couldn't get her out of his mind.

She motioned for him to come closer and whispered. "I'm considering having Open Mic Night once a month or maybe more. Do you think you could get your buddy to man the doors again if I decide to go for it?"

"Probably. Why the change of heart?"

"Everyone had such a great time, and it's really boosted business. Plus, I made a killing. With sales like that, I'll be able to keep this place afloat with no problem."

"Did you ever doubt you could?"

Annika nodded as she handed him the drink. "I hope you have a boring rest of your shift, and please keep quiet about what I said. I don't want to get anyone's hopes up if it doesn't work out."

"Got it. Is it still okay if the guys and I rehearse here tomorrow night?"

"Yes. Be sure to bring Rusty."

"Will do." He spun around and nearly took down the captain. "Sorry. I didn't know you were there."

"No problem. You ready?"

He nodded, took a swallow of his drink and followed his superior to the sidewalk. "Mmm. This is sweet, but I like it. Thanks for stopping."

"Didn't do it for you."

"No?"

"Nope. I wanted my drink, and I wanted to see with

my own eyes if the rumors are true. Annika's face lit when she saw you."

"Baloney. And what rumors?"

"I heard you talking with Jim about her. I think you may have underestimated that lady. She didn't seem bothered at all to see you in uniform."

"I think you may have had a little too much bad coffee from the firehouse and it's affecting your vision. There's nothing between Annika and me except friendship, and it's going to stay that way." Why wouldn't anyone listen to common sense? Even if she was interested in him, he wasn't interested in her. Well, maybe he was, but it didn't matter because it was a bad idea. His last girlfriend wanted to change him, and he was certain Annika would ultimately make him choose between her or fighting fires.

Jim stuck his head out the window. "About time!"

Bryan climbed in and noticed a bakery bag on the seat. "I see you weren't waiting long."

Jim shrugged.

Bryan finished off his drink. Had Annika's face really lit up when she saw him? A tiny spark of hope ignited in spite of himself. The Captain must have imagined it.

# 8

Annika unclasped Rusty's leash and tossed a tennis ball across the grass at the park. "Go get it, boy."

Rusty charged after the toy, chomped it between his teeth then raced back to where she waited. He dropped the ball at her feet.

"Good boy." She squatted down to his level and grabbed the slobbery ball. "Eww." She tossed it again and laughed when Rusty slid to a stop. Bryan was lucky to have such a great dog, and she was lucky to be able to borrow his pet a few nights a week. She'd always wanted a dog, but she didn't have the time to devote to a pet especially now that she had the coffee shop. Her love of animals had prompted her to volunteer at the Second Chances Animal Shelter.

Rusty had his nose in a hole. She clapped her hands. "Come on, boy!"

He raced to her and dropped the toy at her feet again. "Okay. A few more times, then we're taking a walk." She threw the ball. It felt so good to be outside in the sunshine. Children's screams of delight flitted on the light breeze, putting a smile on her face.

She loved the coffee shop, but there was something about being outside on a warm May evening that made her feel alive and happy. After tossing the ball a few more times, she clipped Rusty's leash into place and set out in the direction of the shelter. Maybe Roxanne would be there. She missed visiting with the older woman, like they had when she was a teen.

Things were finally settling into an easy rhythm at the coffee shop. The vandals had stopped tormenting her, and she'd come to terms with having Open Mic Night. In reality, the talent consisted of a lot more than music. There'd been a couple of comedians, an air band, several singers, a few high school garage-type bands, as well as several instrumental solos and groups. The menagerie of talent made it fun—so different from how she felt when at one of her mother's concerts.

A little girl rushed to her. "Can I pet your dog?"

"Sure, but don't run at him."

The child slowed. "I want a dog. We're going to the shelter to pick one out."

"How fun, but I'm pretty sure it's closed for the night." She squatted beside Rusty as the child prattled on telling her all about the kind of dog she wanted.

"It's time to go now, sweetie." The child's mother held out her hand. "Thank the nice lady."

"Thank you for letting me pet your dog," the child said.

"He belongs to a friend, but you're welcome."

The little girl waved with her free hand and skipped along beside her mother.

Annika pulled out her cell phone and gasped. "We need to run, Rusty. Your dad will wonder what happened to us." She struck out at a light jog, but Rusty had a different pace in mind. He raced ahead pulling on the leash and dragging her along behind him. They ran at full steam all the way back to Main Street. Her legs felt like jelly. "Whoa! Stop, boy." She stumbled, and the leash broke free of her hand. The sidewalk came at her fast as she tumbled, scraping her knee and chewing up her palms. She groaned as she pushed up to all fours.

Footsteps raced toward her. She looked up. "Oh, no," she moaned and shakily stood. Her face burned.

Bryan slowed to a walk after she stood. Perfectly behaved on his leash, Rusty trotted beside him.

"You okay?"

"I'm fine." She stuffed her hands into her jeans pockets and took a step toward him. Her knee stung. She was afraid to look, but she suspected the fall had put a hole in her jeans. "I made the mistake of telling Rusty we were going to run." Her stomach lurched. "Did you lock the shop?" It was only a half-block away, but still . . .

"Sorry, no. I stepped outside to see what happened to the two of you and Rusty saw me."

"Don't worry. He just loves you so much he couldn't wait to get back to you. Did you already mop?"

He nodded. "The band finished early tonight." His

gaze swept up and down her body. "Are you sure you're okay? That fall looked like it really hurt."

"It did." She gave him a sheepish smile. "But I'll live. I better get back before someone robs the place."

"Unlikely in Mistletoe Springs."

"Just the same. I'd feel much better having locked doors." She glanced up, catching the last rays of the setting sun. A pinkish-orange hue painted the sky. "Wow, it's really pretty tonight."

"Mmm hmm." His gaze never left her.

She stilled as their eyes met. Why did he have to be so good-looking, kind, and always in the right place at the right time to help her? This man was growing on her— not good. She needed a man content to work in a safe office and listen to music rather than *be* the entertainment. He represented everything she didn't want in a man, yet for some unexplainable reason she was drawn to him like a bee to nectar.

He brushed a loose strand of hair off her cheek. His eyes rested on her lips. She sucked in a breath.

"We should go. You okay to walk now?"

The moment passed, and she let out the breath she'd been holding. "I'm fine."

They walked in silence toward her shop. Her body screamed at her for abusing it. At least the shop was close. A moan escaped her lips.

"You're in pain. I can't let you walk any further." He scooped her up into his arms.

Her heart pitter-pattered at an alarming rate with

every nerve ending in her body aware of his touch. "Put me down. I can walk."

"True and you will, but let me at least help you to the door." He gently set her back on solid ground at the entrance to her shop. His warm breath tickled her cheek. "Next time, tell Rusty to heel. He will listen. I promise." He pushed the door open and stepped into the entry leaving Rusty on the outside. "Does the floor meet your approval?"

She pulled her gaze from his face and examined the shop. "It's great. Thanks. Bye." This man mesmerized her without even trying. She needed to get out more and meet new people. That would clear her head.

He shook his head. "Not so fast. I want to see that knee. I can see a little blood seeping through your jeans."

"Really?" Her gaze shot to her leg that still throbbed. "I'll go get the first aid kit."

"Let me." He gently pushed her onto the nearest seat. "Where is it?"

"Under the register counter."

He strode across the room and disappeared beneath the counter. "Found it." He stood grinning. "I'll have you patched up in no time." He pulled over a chair and sat, then patted his thigh.

Annika gulped. Had she shaved? "You know, I am perfectly capable of applying a bandage."

"I'm sure you are, but I'll rest easier knowing my dog didn't do any real damage, and to know that, I'll have to see for myself." He grinned and patted his leg again.

"Fine." Her face burned as she plopped her leg across his lap then tugged her pant leg to above her knee. It wasn't as bad as she'd imagined. She had a nasty scrape that looked a lot like a rug burn, but it was bleeding a little. "Gross."

He pulled out an alcohol swab and pressed it to the scrape.

She sucked in a hard breath. She had to think about something other than the sting—she was such a baby when it came to blood and pain. Bryan glanced up at her and caught her eye.

"Almost finished."

His gentle touch drew her to him in spite of the circumstances. He had to be the most gentle, kind man she'd ever known, yet there was another side to him as well. The side that was unafraid to go into a burning building, or put himself in danger to save another person. Her heart fluttered at the direction of her thoughts. She had to be careful, or she'd fall for Bryan like she did for his rascally dog. Pain pierced through her thoughts, and she gasped.

"Sorry. I didn't mean to press so hard."

"It's fine." Her throat thickened. She wanted to run and hide in her apartment before she said or did something stupid.

He ripped open a small bandage and applied it to the scrape. "All done."

She scooted the pant leg down and stood. "Thanks."

"You going to be okay going up the stairs on your

own?"

She would have laughed except for the serious look of concern on his face. Instead she took a step back. "I'll be fine." No way did she want him to carry her up the stairs too.

"Okay. I suppose I should head home. Rusty is getting restless." He nodded toward the door where the dog sat intently watching them through the glass.

"Okay. Thanks for the help tonight."

"Help you wouldn't have needed, were it not for my dog."

"Ah, he's a sweetheart. Don't hold it against him. I'm not." She smiled.

He grinned back. "Take care, Annika."

She locked up after him and watched as he and Rusty strode away. With a sigh she turned and headed up the stairs. She caught a glimpse of herself in the hall mirror of her apartment and froze. A woman with a dreamy look in her eyes stared back. She blinked rapidly. "Stop it." She would not fall for a firefighter who was a musician on top of that.

# 9

nnika slapped mayo and a squirt of mustard on a slice of bread then passed it to Lisa to add the rest. They'd received an order for a dozen ham, turkey and cheese sandwiches for noon. Stacy and Trudy, her latest hire, were working the counter up front.

"I haven't seen your handsome firefighter around here in over a week. What's up with that?" Lisa asked.

"He's been in, but after hours." Annika slid the next slice of bread along the marble countertop.

Lisa waggled her brows. "Do tell."

"It's not what you think, so get that look off your face."

"What look?" she asked, now the image of innocence. "I was only wondering why he's coming in after hours."

"His band practices here a few nights a week. In exchange, he mops the floor for me. I take his dog to the park while they rehearse." She always slipped out the minute Bryan showed up and didn't return until she was certain he'd finished for the night.

Lisa frowned. "Well, that's not fun. I thought I spotted a spark between the two of you at the grand re-opening."

The word spark reminded her of fire, which reiterated the reason she was avoiding the man. Bryan had gotten into her head, and she couldn't get him out. If she avoided him long enough, surely her mind would move on. At least that was the plan, but she couldn't avoid him completely. Which made not thinking about him a challenge. "Last sandwich."

"Good. Who are these for anyway?" Lisa asked.

"Stacy took the order, and I didn't think to check. Why?"

"No reason, just curious."

Together they wrapped the sandwiches in plastic wrap then bagged them. In a separate sack she placed twelve red apples and tossed a dozen bags of chips on top to complete the meal. Annika glanced at the clock. "We finished right on time."

Stacy slipped into the kitchen. "Is that order ready? I need it."

"Yes. I'll take care of it, and you can go on break now."

"I won't argue with that. Whew, it's been a busy morning. I don't know what changed, but this place has been hopping since last Saturday. I'm sure glad you hired Trudy. She's great and has picked up things quickly."

"I've noticed. She was a good find for sure. Have a

nice break." Annika grinned as she left the kitchen. Bryan stood at the counter wearing black pants and a polo style shirt with a fire emblem on his left shoulder. Her rebellious heart fluttered. "Hey there, what's up?"

"Not much. Is that my order?"

"*You* ordered a dozen firehouse specials?"

"Yeah. We have training today. I told the guys about your lunch special and they all wanted one." He handed her a hundred dollar bill. Will you add a white chocolate mocha to that too please?"

"You got it." She quickly made his drink. "Will the band be here tonight?"

"No. I forgot to tell you we can't meet tonight. One of the guys has a prior commitment, so we cancelled practice."

"No problem." She glanced toward the window as a cloud covered the sun and dimmed the room, much like Bryan's words had dimmed her spirits. Even though she'd been avoiding spending any extra time with him, she realized now how much she looked forward to seeing him, even if it was only for a moment or two in passing. Her resolve to not fall for him was weakening, but how could she overcome his occupation? She pulled herself from her thoughts and met his eyes. "Have a good one."

"I'll try." He placed the sacks into a cloth bag and strode out.

Lisa sidled up to her. "If I hadn't sworn off men, I might be tempted to ask him out myself."

Annika's stomach knotted. "Down, girl."

Lisa laughed as she grabbed a plastic bin along with a clean rag. A little while later Stacy came back from her break.

Annika pulled off her apron. "You're in charge, Stacy. Lisa's off in fifteen minutes. It will be just you and Trudy. I'm heading out for a couple of hours."

All three of her employees looked at her like she'd just made a major proclamation.

"What?"

Stacy shook her head. "Nothing. But you never take any time away from the shop."

"Then I guess it's about time." She tossed a saucy grin over her shoulder and strode out the front door. Things always slowed after the lunch rush, and she was aching for a visit with Roxanne at the animal shelter. Hopefully her friend would be there.

Sunshine beat down on her head, and she regretted not taking the time to grab sunglasses. A few cumulus clouds flitted in the sky; she'd always enjoyed spotting shapes in the puffy clouds. The one ahead looked like an elephant and another a huge bird.

Annika crossed the street, then ambled left onto Sattler Street. Young children played in the park near the shelter while their mothers chatted on a nearby bench. Had her mom taken her to parks when she was little? Her memories from before the fire that claimed her dad's life were sketchy. Were it not for family photos, she doubted she would even be able to remember his face.

She opened a gate and stepped onto the shelter's

property. Roxanne should be around here someplace. She meandered toward the kennels and spotted the woman with a hose. "Hi there."

Roxanne startled. "Annika! Long time no see." She turned off the water, tossed down the hose, and swept her into a hug. "I've missed your visits."

"I'm sorry about that. The coffee shop has kept me busy, but things are finally feeling under control. I should be able to resume regular volunteering again by next week."

"That's wonderful." Roxanne looped an arm through Annika's. "And speaking of coffee. Are you thirsty? I made fresh-squeezed lemonade."

"My favorite. I can't remember the last time I had some of your lemonade."

Roxanne chuckled. "Come to think of it, neither can I." She stopped beside a patio table. "Have a seat. I'll be right back."

Annika sat on one of the chairs. Her shoulders relaxed, and for the first time in a while she felt at home. The coffee shop and apartment still seemed like her Aunt's place, but the shelter where she'd spent so many hours volunteering when she was younger made her feel warm and content inside. She couldn't imagine Mistletoe Springs without it. They had to raise enough money to fill the gap that losing the grant had left.

"Here we go." Roxanne set a tray on the table. "I hope it's not too tart."

Annika took the glass she offered and sipped. "It's

perfect."

Roxanne eased into the chair beside her. "So what brings you by?"

"Nothing special. I was thinking about our long talks the other day and thought I needed to make a point to visit. It's been way too long since we've had time to chat."

"Indeed it has. I'm glad you came by."

"Any new developments since the emergency meeting?"

"The plans for the Christmas in July fundraiser are moving right along. Have you found our entertainment yet?"

"I have."

Roxanne clapped her hands together. "I knew you wouldn't let us down. Did your mom mind performing for a charity?"

Annika's shoulders stiffened. "I didn't realize you were expecting me to book my mother."

"Oh, well, I just figured you would. If you didn't get your mom, then who?"

"Do you remember Bryan Grant? He volunteered here one summer as a teen and adopted his dog."

"Hmm, the name is familiar, but I can't place him. We've had so many volunteers come and go it's hard to remember them all. Tell me more."

Annika leaned forward, resting her elbows on the table. "His dog is a black Lab named Rusty. He's sweet, but boy can he run fast. Bryan is a firefighter. He's tall, I'm guessing just under six feet, brown hair, fit, and he has a dimple right here." She touched a finger to her right cheek.

Roxanne chuckled. "Unless I'm mistaken I'd say you're smitten with this man."

She gasped. "You are too perceptive for my own good."

Roxanne patted her hand. "You have always worn your heart on your sleeve. That's why the animals love you so much. They sense your kind heart and honesty. Tell me more about Bryan."

"He put out a fire in my kitchen."

"Oh, honey. What happened?"

Annika quickly explained that night. "It was horrible, but Bryan sat in the coffee shop with me for what felt like an hour, just listening to me talk."

"You told him about your dad, didn't you?"

Annika's gaze shot to her older friend's eyes. "How did you know?"

"I could hear it in your voice. He's someone special, and he of all people would understand what you went through that night."

"You're right. He did, and he didn't make me feel bad for being afraid either." Bryan really was a nice man. "If only he didn't fight fires." It was a noble profession and she respected and appreciated what he did, but her heart couldn't take losing another loved one.

"The way I see it is this. Firefighters wear protective gear and are well trained. As long as they follow the rules and abide by their training, they should be as safe as you are each day when you prepare a special coffee."

Annika shrugged. "I suppose so, but accidents happen. Even to trained professionals."

"You know there are no guarantees in life, Annika," Roxanne said gently.

She nodded.

"What I'm trying to say is, that I can see you are struggling with your feelings for this man, and I believe it's because you're afraid. Don't let fear run your life. Fear will destroy you."

"So will a broken heart."

"Hearts mend with time, but fear, if allowed, will take over and consume you, stifling your quality of life."

Annika's throat thickened. Was she allowing fear to control her? She took a long draw from the glass and finished off the lemonade. "Thanks, my friend. You've given me a lot to think about. As long as I'm here is there something I can do to help? I don't need to be back to the shop just yet."

"After I'm done out here, I was going to clean out the bird cages." She raised a brow.

"Consider it done. Well at least one of them done. I've never been very fast at that job, and I should head back in about fifteen minutes." Annika strolled into the room where the birdcages were kept and quickly spotted a pile of precut newspapers that would fit in the tray on the bottom of the cages. She pulled out the tray to replace the newspaper where the droppings piled up. "Hello pretty bird," she said in a sing-song voice, hoping he'd respond.

The parakeet made an unpleasant sound at her.

"Well, excuse me. I only want to clean your cage." She made quick work of the task, then replaced the water in the bottle. The bird squawked at her unmercifully, probably the reason the owner had sent him to the shelter. What a fowl tempered bird. He'd probably been treated unkindly by someone. Thankfully, places like this shelter existed, so unloved animals could find a loving home.

Roxanne walked into the room. "How goes it?"

"Just finishing up, but I'm afraid this is all I have time for."

"I appreciate the help." She started cleaning another cage. "Is it safe to put you on the volunteer schedule, beginning next week?"

"Yes. But only twice a week, and it needs to be in the afternoon after the lunch hour. Maybe one-thirty or two."

"No problem. I'll shoot you a text once I figure out the best time. I'm looking forward to hearing more about this Bryan man too."

Annika quirked a grin. "I hope our conversations are confidential like they've always been."

"Of course."

She quickly washed her hands and waved goodbye. "See you." Now that she'd gotten away from all the chirping and squawking, her mind wandered back to her conversation with Roxanne. Fear had always been an issue for her in many areas of her life. Could it stem from what happened when she was a kid? She'd never put two and two together, but now it gave her pause.

Understanding where the fear came from was one thing. Doing something about it was an entirely different matter, and she wasn't convinced that she could overlook the fact that Bryan put his life on the line every time he went to work.

But what if she could?

# 10

May had rapidly turned into June, Bryan's favorite month of the year. There was something about the end of the rainy season and the warmer temperatures that made him look forward to this month every year. Granted, some years, summer was slow to come and didn't arrive until July, but this year was perfect.

Bryan set the mop and bucket back in the closet, then parked himself on the nearest chair. Annika requested he stay put until she returned with Rusty, but the last couple times she'd been kind of slow getting back.

Too bad he couldn't join her. He'd be happy to walk in the park with the pair. He'd heard from a couple of friends that they'd spotted his dog in the park with her. They said she seemed to really enjoy Rusty. He was glad. He wanted to do something nice for her considering all the stuff she'd had to deal with.

In spite of her past and her obviously conflicted feelings toward him, Annika was fun to be around now that she'd let her guard down with him. He still couldn't figure out what caused the change, but he was glad for it.

He pulled out his smart phone and scrolled through texts, deleting all but one. Mandy, his ex-girlfriend, wanted to get together to talk. What was up with that? He hadn't heard from her in many months and now out of nowhere she'd texted him. He hovered his thumb over delete as the door to the shop swung open.

"Stay, Rusty." Annika slipped the leash handle around the doorknob and closed the door. "We're back," she called loudly.

"Right here."

She jumped and yelped. "I didn't see you."

"I noticed." He stuffed his phone into his pocket and stood. "How was your walk?"

"Nice. Rusty and I played in the park, then sat on the grass and watched the children play. He really likes kids."

He crossed the room noting the flush in her cheeks. Beautiful. "My dog likes everyone. He wasn't always like that. It took a long time to undo the damage his first owner did to him, but he's learned to trust again."

"I had no idea he came from an abusive situation."

He shook his head. "I'm not exactly sure where he came from, but he was clearly not cared for properly. I'm just glad he was still a puppy when they gave him up, so he was still trainable."

"He was probably too much work for his original owners."

"I imagine so. He was a handful, but with lots of love and attention, Rusty has turned into the best dog a man could want."

She grinned. "That's why I like volunteering at the shelter. If not for it and places like it, animals like Rusty would never get that second chance."

"Is that where the name Second Chance Animal Shelter came from?"

"Beats me, but it sounds about right." She leaned against the wall blocking the exit.

A dried up weed or long piece of grass clung to her hair. He stepped closer to her, and reaching out his hand, he gently pulled it from her hair.

She grasped his hand, stilling it, her eyes questioning.

How did he tell her he was attracted to her, but knew there was no future for them, without coming across as a pompous moron? Mandy's text was the reminder he needed to stay strong and not go there—yet he couldn't help the draw he felt toward her. His arms ached to pull her close, and to breathe in deeply the vanilla scent of her hair, to nuzzle her neck—

"Bryan? Are you okay?"

He gently pulled his hand from her grasp. "Fine. Sorry about that. You had this in your hair." He held up the grass. "I'll toss it outside. Have a good one." He strode past her and slid Rusty's leash free. He had to get out of there before he followed through on his thoughts.

"Bye and thanks," she called after him softly.

He lifted a hand without looking back because if he did he was liable to turn around and kiss her.

\* \* \*

Annika stood at the window and watched Bryan hustle down the street with his dog. She shivered, wondering at what had just taken place between them. At least it felt like something.

She locked up then climbed the stairs to her apartment. There was no denying she liked Bryan, and unless she was mistaken, he liked her too and not just because she let his band use her shop.

She kicked off her tennis shoes and sprawled out on the couch. She missed Rusty already. It would sure be nice to have a pet to come home to. This place was too quiet and lonely. Maybe that was why she hadn't minded the long hours in the shop, but the place was running smoothly now, especially since adding Open Mic Night. She had her help well trained and the schedule worked out, which left her time for a life.

But what did she want to do with her free time? She couldn't hide out at the animal shelter every afternoon. Well, she could, but that wasn't what she wanted, plus what happened if the shelter couldn't raise the funds they needed and ended up closing? She'd be lonelier than ever. She needed a life outside of work and volunteering! She rolled off the couch and padded into the kitchen avoiding the stove, which still needed to be replaced, and instead reached into the fridge for a carton of peach Greek yogurt. She hopped onto the counter and studied her apartment. With a fresh coat of paint and new furniture, she could make this place her own. That's how she'd spend her free time in the afternoons—making over her apartment—but she'd need some muscle to move out the old and bring in the new. Good thing she knew a strong man.

# 11

Bryan stood near the bay doors to the fire station with his hands stuffed in his pocket. Mandy insisted on meeting him here. He wasn't even on duty. He ran his free hand through his hair.

A black hatchback pulled into the parking lot. Mandy sat behind the wheel. She stepped out. Nothing. He felt nothing! Relief surged through him. He'd dreaded seeing her again, afraid it would bring up all the hurt and old feelings.

Mandy ran a hand down her black skirt and then through her short dark hair. Hair he knew for a fact felt like silk, but he no longer had the urge to run his fingers through it. Instead he wished Annika was the woman walking toward him wearing a huge smile.

"Thanks for meeting me, Bryan. I realize I had no right to ask."

"You're welcome. What's going on?"

She held out her left hand. A large diamond sparkled in the morning sunlight. "I'm engaged."

"Congratulations!" The word slipped from his lips surprising him, but he meant it. "I'm glad you found someone who makes you happy."

"You made me happy too, Bryan." She rested a hand on his forearm. "I've done a lot of soul searching since we broke up, and I wanted to apologize for the way I treated you. I never should have led you on the way I did, and I'm sorry. I knew you'd never give up fire fighting. Like you said, it's in your DNA."

Mandy could not have surprised him more if she'd slapped him on the face. "Wow. Thanks, Mandy." The tension in his shoulders eased a little. "I wasn't crazy about meeting you today, but I'm glad I did."

She grinned. "Me too. So, are you seeing anyone?"

"No. I've decided staying single is best for me."

She sucked in a breath. "I don't agree. You're a passionate man, and you need to find a special someone to share all that love you have to give."

His face warmed. "That sounds like a song lyric."

"Feel free to use it." She moved back a step. "I should go. I accomplished what I came to town to do. I wish you all the best, Bryan." She blew him a kiss then slid into her car.

A weight felt like it'd been lifted. Not in the mood to go home, he set out for Main Street Java. That place always had someone around to visit with, plus that white chocolate mocha drink had become a favorite. He lengthened his stride, propelled by the need to see Annika. Mandy's words struck a chord. He really wasn't created to be alone. Maybe Annika wasn't the woman for him considering her extreme fear of fire, but they'd become friends over the past few months, and he enjoyed her company.

He pushed into the shop and paused, allowing his eyes to adjust to the indoor lighting. Annika was nowhere in sight. His stomach sunk. Lisa stood at the counter.

"Good morning, Bryan. Would you like your usual?"

He nodded and pulled out his wallet. "Where's the boss lady?"

"Frosting cinnamon rolls. Stacy makes them fresh at home, and we bake them off here. Have you tried one yet?"

"Nope, but they sure smell good."

"Hold on one minute." Lisa disappeared into the kitchen and came back a moment later with a small plate piled with small chucks of cinnamon rolls. She poked a toothpick into one and handed it to him. "Taste."

He popped it into his mouth. Warm goodness exploded over his taste buds. "I'll take one of those too."

"I thought you might. Be right back."

Stacy had his drink ready at the other end of the counter.

He strolled over and grasped the warm cup. "How are things going here, Stacy?" Stacy had been a fixture in this town for longer than him and they'd become friends over the years.

"Really well. Annika has good business sense. She's added a few things to the menu that have been a big hit too."

He grinned. "Do you mean your cinnamon rolls?"

She beamed a wide smile. "Yep. We started off selling them only once a week. They were such a hit, Annika's upped them to twice a week now. I'm the one holding her back from putting them on the menu everyday." She lowered her voice, "I don't want to be up early every morning making cinnamon rolls. Twice a week is plenty." She chuckled. "Now that the word is getting out, people are starting to come in just for the rolls."

"That's great. Congratulations."

Movement in his peripheral vision grabbed his attention. He turned and spotted Annika approaching with a plate in hand. A warm smile lit her face. He stepped toward her.

"I believe this is for you." She handed him the roll.

"Thanks." He reached for his wallet.

"Keep your money."

Giving him drinks had become a regular occurrence, but she didn't usually comp him food. "Do you have time to join me?"

"Sure."

Stacy winked at him. "Here you go, boss. I made your favorite. I figured you were due for a break."

Annika grinned and shook her head. "Now you're a mind reader as well as a cinnamon roll maker extraordinaire. Thanks."

He led the way to a window seat. "You're looking especially lovely this morning, Annika."

She blinked surprised eyes at him. "Ah, thanks? You've never complimented me on my looks before."

"Really? I'll have to work on that." He forked a bite of the roll into his mouth to hide his embarrassment. Why had he said that? His mouth was running ahead of his brain. Annika always looked good, but for some reason her peach completion radiated today. *Ugh.* Mandy's words were getting to his head. He needed to get a grip before he said something stupid.

He really cared for this woman and wanted to be with her. For the first time since breaking up with Mandy, he didn't care about a broken heart. He was willing to take a risk. Annika was worth it. "Do you have plans for this evening?"

"Uh. No. I guess not. You?"

He couldn't believe what he was about to do, but why not? "That all depends on you. I thought about taking Rusty to the park and then maybe playing a game of tennis."

"With who?"

He raised a brow. "You?"

She rested her elbows on the table interlacing her fingers. "I suppose I could be persuaded to dig out my tennis racket. But I'm not very good."

"Me neither. What time works for you?"

"Seven thirty?"

"Sounds good." He finished off the rest of the roll and finished up the mocha and stood. "I'll stop by here and we can walk over together."

"Okay. See you then."

* * *

Annika rushed up the stairs to her apartment after work. She only had ten minutes to get ready for her "date" with Bryan. Did playing tennis qualify as a date? She hadn't thought so when she said yes, but according to Lisa and Stacy it was a date.

She quickly changed into comfortable shorts and a white T-shirt, then ran to the coat closet and yanked open the door. A cluttered mess greeted her. She groaned. How was she supposed to find her racket in this mess? A skateboard she'd never had the heart to get rid of rested against one corner, several boxes filled the center of the floor and the top shelf was stacked high with shoe boxes, knickknacks, games, and who knew what else. Was that the handle of her racket peeking out between the boxes up top? She reached on tiptoe and pulled. It wouldn't budge. She pulled harder and it moved slightly. "Oh my goodness. This is nuts." Bryan would be there any minute. She reached up and yanked hard. Boxes flew off the shelf, one smacking her in the head on its way to the floor. She rubbed her head. "What a mess."

"Are you okay?"

She caught her breath and whirled around to find Bryan standing in her doorway.

"I knocked, then a I heard a crashing sound. I was afraid you were in trouble."

Her face burned as she held up the tennis racket. "It was buried."

He chuckled. "Would you like help cleaning that up?" He motioned to the boxes and games strewn on the floor at her feet.

"Thanks. I could use your height." It was a wonder the man felt safe in her presence considering he witnessed her klutziest moments. She handed him boxes as he re-stacked them above. "I think maybe I'll store the racket down here."

"Good idea." He stacked the last box then stepped away from the closet. "You ready for some tennis?"

She nodded and followed him out the door and down the stairs leading to the alley. They set out side by side toward the tennis courts. "Now that I'm fully staffed, I'm going to start working on my apartment in the afternoons. Could I persuade you to help me out? I'll provide pizza and soda." She held her breath.

"I think that could be arranged if you're willing to work around my schedule at the firehouse. What'd you have in mind?"

"A fresh coat of paint. New wall art and furniture, a new stove, new window coverings."

"Things at the shop must be improving. I remember you were worried about finances not all that long ago."

"It's holding its own now, plus my aunt left me a little money to spend however I wanted. What do you say?"

"I happen to be handy, so count me in. Who else is

helping?"

"Uh . . . I'm still working on that. Most of my friends work during my free time, so . . ."

"That's fine. We could do it ourselves."

They stopped at the fence that surrounded the tennis court where another couple was already playing. She shielded her eyes from the sun and looked at the other court—full. " I didn't consider the courts might be busy."

"Me neither. We could sit and wait."

She shrugged. "Why not? I don't have anything better to do."

He chuckled. "Oh, nothing at all. That apartment of yours will revamp itself, I suppose."

She nudged him with her shoulder. "You know what I meant. But as long as I have your undivided attention, what color should I paint the walls?"

"Easy. Something neutral."

"Like a dove gray?"

"Yeah. That would look nice with your floors. Not that I'm an expert, but I know what I like. I guess that counts for something at least."

"Sure does." She grinned. They could sit here all night discussing paint colors and she'd be happy. Being with Bryan warmed her insides, plus she did not look forward to showing her lack of talent on the court.

The couple who'd been playing tennis a moment ago walked off the court. "It's all yours."

"Thanks," Bryan said.

Annika's stomach knotted and her palms grew moist.

Saying she wasn't very good at tennis was an understatement. She wanted to impress Bryan, but that would never happen on the tennis court.

He served. She swung and missed.

He served again. She ran to the ball and made contact, but with her wrist instead of the racket. Pain radiated up her arm and to make matters worse the ball didn't make it over the net. After twenty minutes or so Bryan approached the net and motioned her to him.

She jogged up to him. "What's up?"

"You don't play tennis, do you?"

"Not very well." She scrunched up her nose. "I'm better at throwing Rusty's ball, than making contact with a tennis ball."

He grinned. "Fair enough. Do you want to learn?"

"I'm afraid I'm hopeless. I lack hand-eye coordination."

"Oh," he let the word draw out. "Is that what you call it." A twinkle lit his eyes. "Let me help you. You're not as bad as you think."

"Liar." She chuckled.

He hopped the net then stood beside her. "You need to hold the racket like this." He held his in front of them, then set it down and adjusted her hand on the racket. "Whenever the ball is to your right this is how you hold it." He reached for her other hand and placed it on the racket too. "This is how I like to hold it when it goes to my right. It gives me a little more power and control."

The skin where he touched sizzled. She was in big

trouble. "Thanks. I think I have it now, but it's getting a little dark."

"How about we call it a night?"

"Sounds good to me." They strolled toward her place, finally stopping in that alley at the entrance to her apartment. "Walk me up?"

"Sure."

She unlocked the door and climbed the stairs groaning. "It's times like this, I wish my apartment was on the ground level. I can't believe I'm already sore."

"You can make it. Just a few more steps."

Panting, she stopped outside her door and turned to face him. "In spite of my terrible ability at tennis, I had fun tonight."

"Me too."

"Well, I should go in." She'd never wanted to kiss a man as much as she did right at this moment, but it would be a bad idea for both of them if she did. "Goodnight, Bryan."

"'Night." His eyes bore into her as though he could read her mind.

She hurriedly tried to stick the key into the lock. Her hand shook and kept missing.

His warm palm covered hers and guided the key into the hole. "Sleep well, Annika," he said softly before backing away. "I'll make sure the alley door locks on my way out."

She nearly floated into her apartment in spite of her sore body. Sleep would be a long time coming tonight.

Her mind would never shut down. Her hand still tingled where he'd grasped it. What was she going to do? The more time she spent with Bryan, the more she wanted to be around him. And the more she was with him, the fonder she grew of him. Which scared her silly.

# 12

The day before the shelter's fundraiser, Annika loaded the roller with dove gray paint. She'd tried several sample patches, but ended up with her original choice. It'd been a challenge finding time to actually do this, but this afternoon she hoped to paint all the walls in her apartment, minus the bedrooms and bathroom.

Bryan stood a few feet away, and Rusty sat on a soft doggie bed, Bryan had brought over. Good thing Rusty was well behaved. She could only imagine the mess if he wasn't.

Bryan had become a very good friend. She'd stopped avoiding him when his band was practicing and they'd spent a lot of time visiting over decaf coffee many times into the wee hours of the morning.

"Is the band ready for tomorrow?"

"As ready as we'll ever be. I have to admit I'm nervous."

"Don't be. You guys are great. And your rendition of "Joy to the World" is fantastic. I've never heard it performed with so much rock influence."

"Thanks! I'm partial to "Jingle Bells," but I like that one too."

She nodded. "Yep. That's a good one." She was impressed with the way the group had taken traditional Christmas songs and re-worked them to be high energy songs. Plus they'd changed some of the lyrics to include the different animals up for adoption.

She applied the paint to the wall that faced the alley while Bryan worked beside her. Paint splattered into her hair and onto her cheek. "Scoot that way." She motioned further down on the wall. "You're painting *me*." She pointed to her face then wiped it with the back of her hand.

"Sorry about that. Here let me help." He pulled a rag from his pocket and dabbed at her cheek. "Uh-oh."

Wetness covered her cheek. She reached a hand to her face and touched the spot, then pulled her hand away. "Bryan," she dragged out his name. "How could you?"

"It was an accident. I forgot I'd wiped my hands on it after I touched the wet paint on the wall." He chuckled. "Sorry, it's just that you look adorable when you're annoyed."

She narrowed her eyes. "Adorable, huh?" As if her hand had a mind of its own, she rolled paint across his stomach.

His eyes widened. "You didn't just do that."

She scrunched her nose. "I think so."

A gleam lit his eyes. With perfect wrist action he

flung splatters of paint at her.

"Oh, so that's how you are." Laughter bubbled up. "This was fun, but I won't have enough paint if we keep this up."

Rusty barked.

"See. Even your dog agrees."

"I think he'd agree with this too. You're pretty wonderful. Paint and all."

Annika's pulse pounded in her ears. "I think you're pretty wonderful too."

"I'm glad." Taking the roller from her hands, he placed it into the paint tray then took her hands. "Mind if I ask you a question?"

"I don't think so." His reflective tone unnerved her. They'd been getting along well and had spent a good deal of time together lately, but she sensed something was up.

"Thanks. I was wondering if your fear of fire would keep you from having a relationship with someone like me."

*Whoa!* "If you'd asked me that question the evening my stove caught fire I'd have said yes, but now . . .To be honest, getting past my fears and not allowing them to control me has been something I've been working on. Plus a good friend pointed out that you are well trained and prepared to fight fires." Her stomach felt like a jumble of nerves.

"You have a wise friend. How's getting past your fear going?" The tender look in his eyes about undid her.

She licked her lips. "Better than I even thought possible." More than anything she wanted to feel his arms around her. Yearned to be held by him, to know if his heart beat as wildly as hers. She could no longer deny her affection for the man. She wanted to be with him all the time. Her heart skipped whenever he walked into the coffee shop and most importantly she just now realized, it no longer mattered to her that he fought fires. After her talk with Roxanne at the shelter, she'd worked hard to put her faith in God and to stop being afraid all the time. Gradually the fear had ebbed.

"I think you are the most precious person I've ever met. I can't get enough of being with you." He drew her closer.

She caught her breath. Her pulse pounded in her ears. His minty breath tickled her cheek. Heady with anticipation she closed her eyes.

He cradled her neck with one hand and drew close, hesitating slightly. "You have no idea how much I want to kiss you."

She closed the distance. "What's stopping you?" she asked softly.

His warm lips caressed hers. He held her tighter, deepening the kiss until her knees turned to mush.

She pulled back, immediately missing the contact, but knowing it was necessary.

She ran her thumb across the dimple in his right cheek. "I've always had a thing for dimples, especially yours."

He grinned wider. "You do realize they're a genetic flaw?"

"Perfection is overrated." She loved this man and

didn't care what his job was or even that he was a musician. God made him to be exactly who he was.

"What are you thinking?" He stepped back ever so slightly.

"That you're exactly the person God created you to be. Passionate, hard working, overflowing with love, generous . . ."

"And don't forget, the man who loves *you*. I think I've loved you since that day we first met years ago at the animal shelter. You were cleaning out a dog kennel and dropped the hose, but the spray nozzle was stuck and sprayed you in the face. You stood there and laughed."

Electricity zipped through her body. "I didn't know anyone saw that, but it was pretty funny."

He caressed her cheek with the back of his hand. "So you think there is a future for us considering your fire phobia?"

She titled her head into his touch. "I do. Like I said, I've been working on my fear and I've given it to the Lord. I'm sure there will be times when I freak out on you, but just know it's only because I love you."

"You do?"

"Oh, yeah."

He wrapped his arms around her and lifted her to his eye level. "I can't wait to see what the future holds for us." His lips found hers once more before he lowered her to her feet.

—The End—

# About the Author

Kimberly Rose Johnson is a multi-published author and soon to be empty-nester. She lives in the Pacific Northwest with her husband and their yellow lab. Kimberly enjoys long walks, chocolate, and mochas, not necessarily in that order.


You may subscribe to my newsletter at
kimberlyrjohnson.com
Amazon follow: http://amzn.to/2jpZj1C
Facebook: www.facebook.com/KimberlyRoseJohnson

# Books by
# Kimberly Rose Johnson

### Melodies of Love

*A Love Song for Kayla*

*An Encore for Estelle*

*A Waltz for Amber* (Coming soon!)

### Sunriver Dreams

*A Love to Treasure*

*A Christmas Homecoming*

*Designing Love*

### Wildflower B&B Romance Series

*Island Refuge*

*Island Dreams*

*Island Christmas*

*Island Hope*

### Contemporary Inspirational Romance Collection

*In Love and War*

www.ingramcontent.com/pod-product-compliance
Lightning Source LLC
Chambersburg PA
CBHW051304170626
46809CB00004B/1771